Return to Portovenere

Annette Creswell

Pharos Books

All rights reserved. No part of this publication may be reproduced, stored in a retrieval system, or transmitted, in any form, or by any means, electronic, mechanical, photocopying, recording or otherwise, without the prior permission of the publishers.

Hardcover ISBN: 978-93-95862-38-7
Paperback ISBN: 978-93-95862-37-0
eBook ISBN: 978-93-95862-32-5

©Publisher

Publisher: Pharos Books (P) Ltd.
Plot No.-55, Main Mother Dairy Road
Pandav Nagar, East Delhi-110092
Phone: 011-40395855, +4049916623
WhatsApp: +91 8368220032
E-mail: sales@pharosbooks.in
Website: www.pharosbooks.in
First Edition: 2023

Printed By: Sushma Book Binding House, Okhla Industrial Area, Phase II, New Delhi-110020

RETURN TO PORTOVENERE
By Annette Creswell

CONTENTS

Chapter 1 5
Chapter 2 10
Chapter 3 16
Chapter 4 20
Chapter 5 28
Chapter 6 32
Chapter 7 43
Chapter 8 50
Chapter 9 63
Chapter 10 68
Chapter 11 79
Chapter 12 82
Chapter 13 86
Chapter 14 95
Chapter 15 99
Chapter 16 107
Chapter 17 114
Chapter 18 120
Chapter 19 129
Chapter 20 138
Epilogue 149

1
CHAPTER

1985

As the ferry stopped at Riomaggiore, the sky echoing the cerulean colour of the sea, I knew it would not be long before my eyes would alight on the bay of poets and that jewel in the crown of Cinque Terre, Portovenere. I was on a pilgrimage for my mother whose ashes I would scatter onto this sea, the sea in which she had bathed in those halcyon days before the Second World War when la dolce vita was embraced. Rounding the bend, my eyes beheld the scene which mother had described; the ancient church of San Pietro standing sentinel on the promontory, Byron's grotto, albeit collapsed, under the steep rock wall, and the village spilling down to the water below. I now knew why mother, Byron and the other poets had been so entranced by the magic of this place and Byron's tribute immediately came to my mind: "Italia, oh Italia! Thou who hast the fatal gift of beauty." We glided to the wharf and, gathering my suitcase, I joined the throng who like me were impatient to explore this beauteous destination at which we had arrived.

I hailed a taxi which the driver informed me was one of only two servicing the village and we headed to my accommodation. It was a stone cottage about twenty minutes from the Cinque Terre trail, far from the madding crowd, and would be my home for the next few months. My mother had told me she had stayed here many years ago and wished for me to do so. It was with amazement that I discovered that not only was it still cleaving to the earth, but had been listed as a short-term rental.

'Grazie,' I said handing the driver the fare. The route we had taken had been circuitous, the road taking us along Via Cappelini then winding around and up through the caruggi until eventually arriving at the panoramic view of the ocean and the impending sunset. I wheeled my bag along the path and finding the key under the terracotta pot which had been left by the agent let myself into the cottage. It was basically the same as mother had described. Apart from some modernity such as a new sink, a dishwasher and a television with a VCR in the corner of the lounge-room, the old wooden beams still held up the low ceiling and the window shutters served to keep the cottage cool. I thrust them open letting in the waning light and the sea air to refresh the room. The agent had kindly left a few basic supplies to tide me over until I could organise a proper shop. There was a basket of rolls on the old pine table together with tea bags and coffee and the refrigerator contained milk, eggs, butter, parma ham and a hunk of cheese. Satisfied that I would have enough food to sustain me for at least a couple of days I made my way into the bedroom.

Sitting on the bed I was suddenly overwhelmed by fatigue. I kicked off my shoes and lay down. The last few months had been mentally and physically exhausting. My mother's condition had deteriorated to the point that it had been a blessing when in the confines of Trinity Hospice she had finally succumbed. The specialist had opined that the cancer which had ravaged her lungs had been due to the numerous cigarettes she had smoked throughout her life. The people with whom she had associated in the twenties had all been smokers when Turkish cigarettes were de rigeur along with magnums of champagne in London and brown sherry in Oxford. These people, the "The Bright Young Things," the sons and daughters of the aristocracy and some of the middle classes revelled in shocking society with their outrageous behaviour. They held numerous parties; Russian parties,

Wild West parties, half naked parties, and parties where one had to dress as someone else. There were parties in flats and lofts, windmills, ships and swimming baths. Treasure hunts were conducted on public transport creating mayhem amongst the everyday commuters and the country lanes would echo to the sounds of roaring motors and caterwauling passengers intent on claiming their prize.

During her better moments, mother used to enthral me with some of what had gone on in those days, and my life seemed to pale in comparison, me, a lowly librarian in a Fulham flat, with hardly any social life to speak of. My circle of friends was minimal and the few sexual encounters I experienced had left me disillusioned and confused. However, I enjoyed travelling, hence my decision to come abroad on this pilgrimage to lay mother to rest. I had long service owing to me so this was an opportune time to go. I would spend time here at Portovenere where I hoped to unearth things about my mother, things to which she had vaguely alluded in the final period of her life.

'Georgia,' she had whispered towards the end taking my hand in hers the hand now papery, scribbled with the wrinkles and spots of age.

'I want you to scatter me about on the sea at Portovenere. There is a stone cottage on the cliff. Stay there, it would mean so much.' She dropped my hand onto the sheet and her eyes closed as her breathing became shallower. I sat and looked at her my mother now not long for this world and wondered why she had particularly mentioned this cottage, and in her dying breaths insisted I stay there.

As I reached adulthood, I had a feeling there had always been something about her, the way she was with me and my father, her depressive moods, her aloofness, the constant smoking and need to escape from the family home away to the surrounding hills and beaches of Suffolk. The first time she had disappeared the police had been summoned, my father, after much searching unable to locate her. She was ultimately found sitting on the beach at Aldeburgh staring out to sea. Mother was not of the aristocracy, however her life was considered to be privileged. The only child of Edward and Florence Banks, my mother was cared for by nanny Watts as was the custom in those Victorian days. They lived in the fashionable suburb of Chelsea in a Georgian townhouse from which my grandfather would leave in a Hansom Cab to Lombard Street where he was the manager of the bank. My grandmother was rather an austere opinionated woman and preferred the company of her female friends rather than her husband. Many card games and luncheons saw her in attendance as well as races at Ascot and other country meetings at which she would hold forth about the state of the nation and anything else with which she disagreed.

My journey to Portovenere had commenced in Rome to which I had flown direct and stayed at a bed and breakfast near St Peter's Basilica. From there I had easy access to the Sistine Chapel so I could admire the splendour of Michelangelo's art. Fortunately, as it was the end of summer there were no great hordes of tourists unlike the last time I had visited on holiday with a girl friend when the heat and the crowds had been unbearable. This time, with the chapel nearly empty, I was able to absorb its wonders and pray in relative peace for the repose of my parents' souls and for assistance in my mission in Portovenere.

Venice was my next port of call. With its unique canals and mazes of narrow alleyways filled with tiny shops it would always be one of my most favourite cities. I had caught the train from Rome and had booked a hotel near San Marco square. After unpacking a few clothes, I wandered into the maelstrom of camera clicking tourists and the flocks of pigeons which always descended on this site. Its beauty never failed to astound me no matter how many times I visited, even the birds added to its charm. The portals of Cafe Florian drew me in, the liveried waiter ushering me to a table in the corner. It may have been the table at which Dickens or perhaps Byron sat as this cafe had hosted many artists since its opening in 1720.

'Un caffe por favore' I said as the waiter hovered beside me. He glided away and it was only a few minutes later when he returned with a silver tray bearing my coffee, a jug of milk and a pot of hot water. Nothing had changed. It was as though the place was in a time warp I thought as I sipped my coffee and watched the multitudes pass by the window. That evening before dinner I walked to Harry's Bar for a farewell drink. It would have to be a Bellini I determined, as I wended my way along the alleyways, as that was the cocktail which had been invented in this bar. The prices certainly had increased since the last time I was here as my eyes detected the 6000 lira written on the bill. It was the price one had to pay if one wished to visit this erstwhile place, the most famous bar in Venice. I decided to have a bite to eat there as well as I did not possess the stamina to locate another venue. There was a pain behind my eye which I knew to be the start of a migraine so, after consuming a mushroom omelette and my drink I made my way back to my hotel. I swallowed some tablets, undressed and crawled into bed. I slept fitfully through the night, my thoughts turning to tomorrow's journey, my final destination, Portovenere.

CHAPTER 2

The first rays of sunlight stole into the room. Last night in my weariness I had neglected to close the shutters however, it pleased me to have the light as I could not abide dark places. I lay there for a few minutes trying to process my journey so far, this journey which seemed to be just commencing. I had to plan the scattering of mother's ashes and find an appropriate place at which to do so. I wanted it to be meaningful, something of which she would approve. I had come to terms with her behaviour as I realised she must have had some sort of disorder in her psyche as I had studied psychology at university and had read about cases such as hers. There must have been something in her life which had triggered her condition. I surmised maybe it was how she had been brought up. Her mother had not bestowed much maternal love towards her daughter and the nanny seemed to be rather a curmudgeon as well.

My father's ashes had not been scattered as his Catholicism was not in favour of cremation. His body was buried in St Mary's Church cemetery Thorpeness, the village in which he had married my mother and where we had lived. Dear dad, dying from a coronary occlusion at his solicitor's practice. He had been always there for us, always trying his best when mother's moods were at their worst, trying to placate and cajole her even while she spurned him on many occasions. These times would render me fearful that something terrible would eventuate and I would run to my bed and take refuge under the sheets until mother's fury was spent and things returned to normal. I used to wonder why she married my father as his love and devotion did not seem to be reciprocated over the years. There were no outward displays of affection towards him but I thought, like many unions, the passion had evaporated after the first flush of romance had waned.

His funeral had been dismal. I had hoped to farewell him in sunshine which I thought was what he deserved, a beautiful sunny cloudless day, but it was not to be. The rain had been relentless as we stood about the gravesite under sodden umbrellas, our shoes sinking into the mud and the shrieking wind drowning out the intonations of the priest. At least it also drowned out my sobs and distracted the mourners from my mother's lack of emotion as the casket was lowered into the ground. In deference to father's Irish heritage, my aunt and I had organised a real Irish wake at the village pub however, pleading illness, mother had left early to take to her bed. It was a few days after that she was admitted to hospital with a chest infection resulting in the diagnosis of lung cancer.

I had brought with me a box of old photos which I had discovered at the back of mother's wardrobe when I had been clearing out the house and had planned to go through them whilst staying at the cottage. During the clear out I had unearthed all manner of things. There were drawers full of plastic cling wrap and gifts which people had given her still in their original wrapping. There were old handkerchiefs with her initials EB embroidered on them as well as her old school ties and awards for hockey games, debating and literature. As I went through her wardrobe to see what could be given to charity or thrown out I detected her perfume, Arpege, her favourite. But there was also another smell, ephemeral, lingering among her dresses and coats. It took me awhile to detect what it was. It was not like the odour of nursing homes or geriatric facilities which is usually urine and antiseptic. This was a different smell; it was of old age, old skin. I felt as though part of mother was still here hidden in the folds and creases of her clothes and I found it difficult to proceed with the clearing out. Up until now I had not really perceived her to be an old woman as she had retained her youthful looks right until the end. I had not really grieved for her as she and I had not been close but she was my mother, the one who had given birth to me. I buried my face in one of her dresses allowing my tears to dampen it. Then the catharsis over, I continued sorting, deciding to keep a navy jacket which I thought would fit me if I did not do up the buttons, and also a black leather handbag inside of which were a used theatre ticket and a powder compact. As I gathered up the rest of her clothes to send to charity I thought of my own mortality. Would someone go through my things when I had died of old age and would they also be aware of that smell peculiar to it?

My rumbling stomach alerted me it was time for breakfast. I had not realised how hungry I was as I devoured two eggs with ham and a roll. I was pouring a second cup of tea when there was a knock on the door. I wondered who could it be so early although, glancing at the clock on the wall, it was not as early as I thought. Pulling my gown tightly around me and running a hand through my hair I walked to the door.

'Buongiorno, signora,' said the leprechaunish vision before me taking off his cap. His leathery face attested to many years exposure to the Mediterranean sun and he looked about one hundred years old.

'Buongiorno' I replied.

'Scusami, I am gardener' he said.

'Oh, I see. Have you come to do some work now?'

'Si, I clip the bushes and rake leaves.'

'Oh, ok. How often do you come?'

'Every fortnighta.'

I looked around the garden and could not discern any leaves on the ground and the bushes appeared to be neat and tidy. I assumed he was contracted by the agency and kept arriving even though there was not much gardening to be done. By the look of him he probably needed the money.

'I was just having a cup of tea. Would you like a cup too, or maybe a caffe?' I ventured knowing that Italians prefer their morning espressos. The corners of his eyes crinkled into a smile and without hesitation he scuttled into the kitchen and had settled himself into the chair and placed his worn cap on the table.

'I have not any coffee to make you an espresso, I'm afraid. I only have instant. I just arrived last night and I have only the basics.' I told him as I took a mug off the hook under the cupboard.

'Grazie, signora. No problema. I will have instanta.'

I put the jug on to boil then made a fresh tea for me and an instant coffee for my guest.

'You here on the holiday?' He asked as he slurped his coffee which he had liberally laced with four teaspoons of sugar. I noted this and thought about all the warnings we are given about the dangers of consuming excess sugar. It did not seem to have had any effect on this fellow.

'Yes, I suppose you could say that,' I replied.

'English lady, all alone,' he mused.

'Yes, that's me.'

'First time Portovenere?' he asked.

'Yes, it is, and from what I saw yesterday from the ferry it is a beautiful place.'

'Si, I live here longa time. Many people visit, many poets.'

'Yes,' I replied, 'This place seemed to be very inspirational for lots of creative people.'

He quickly slurped the rest of his coffee then got up to leave.

'Grazie for caffe, signora.'

'Oh, you are welcome. Maybe next time you come you can have another.'

Manifesting a little bow, he took off at speed vanishing into a dilapidated shed in the corner of the garden exiting with secateurs in one hand and a rake in the other. I did not want him to see me watching so I shut the door and let him get on with whatever he was doing. What a funny little man I mulled, as I collected the dirty dishes and mugs and placed them in the dishwasher. Suddenly, an overwhelming feeling of sadness and loneliness overcame me and I was tempted to go outside and ask him to come back. It was a while since I had actually sat with someone and conversed, apart from perfunctory exchanges with hotel staff and the tourists I had come across on my journey. I supposed that was why I had enjoyed his company. He seemed such a likeable person, a grandfatherly figure sitting as he did in this cosy kitchen as though he belonged here. Turning on the dishwasher I thought about my ancestors. My maternal great grandfather was Scottish and had lived with his wife in a cold, draughty pile at Dornoch in the highlands. He was rather wealthy although being a Scot was frugal with his money and was known to practically live in a patched pair of plus fours and a holey jumper in which he would stride daily in all weathers over the highlands, his old basset hound running faithfully behind him. Mother would tell me whenever she visited she always felt hungry as their dinners consisted of leftovers from the day before. 'Waste not want not' was the refrain as my mother's look of distaste would not go unnoticed as she sat at the table expected to consume the cold fatty lamb and cabbage before her. Often her grandfather used to take her to see the witch's stone which commemorated the last witch who was burnt in Dornoch in 1722 and mother would be threatened with the same fate whenever her wilfulness came to the fore. To these threats grandmother would always respond, 'Ah yer aff yer heid yer auld coot!' However, her threats tended to be more normal, 'I'm going ta skelp yer wee behind!' whenever there were signs of misbehaviour. I had wondered if her grandfather's dire warnings had left a lasting impression on mother's psyche as hearing that sort of thing when a youngster would have been quite disturbing. My grandparents on my father's side came from Tipperary in Ireland. Driven from their farm due to the potato famine they had emigrated to England and settled in Lavenham in Suffolk where they tended sheep for one of the gentry and finally succeeded in having their own little farm where they brought up seven children. My thoughts reverted to the old gardener. He probably was used to being invited in by the various tenants who had stayed in this cottage over the years. It occurred to me then he might even have known my mother. I determined to find out the next time he came and somewhat buoyed by this thought, returned to the bedroom where I dressed, placed mother's urn on the dressing table and finished unpacking.

CHAPTER 3

'Be careful, Georgia, the rocks are slippery,' Maria warned.

'Grazie, yes, I will.' I replied as I picked my way carefully across the black volcanic rocks washed by the sea. I was carrying the urn containing mother's ashes and accompanying me was Maria the granddaughter of the old gardener, Piero and also Piero himself who had insisted on coming with me on this solemn occasion. He was the one leading us on, his little sprightly form darting from rock to rock as he was used to this place, having fished around these craggy cliffs numerous times over the years. A friendly relationship had developed between him and me since that first morning four weeks ago when I had made him coffee, leading to a meeting with Maria and her husband, Marko. I already felt like one of them being invited to their home which was in one of the narrow caruggi which criss-crossed the village, there to partake of delicious pasta and copious amounts of prosecco. I had posed the question to Piero on one of those nights, if he had ever met my mother. He had pondered the question but was unable to remember. He had vaguely recalled some English people around the village in the twenties sunning themselves under umbrellas on deck chairs at the beach and on the rocks. He said they had been easy to spot with their milky white skin untouched by the sun, so unlike the inhabitants of the village whose skin was a darker shade.

They had taken me to see the medieval church of San Pietro, the one I had observed on the promontory as the ferry approached the day I arrived. It was in that tiny stone church today the three of us had lit candles and said prayers for the repose of mother's soul before making our way around the cliff path above the grotto of Byron who had lived here and swum in this sea all those years ago around the same time as mother. I intuited this would be the appropriate location at which to scatter her ashes.

As Maria and Piero made the signs of the cross I unscrewed the lid of the urn and the ashes were taken by the wind and down onto the roiling water. I could scarcely believe that she was now gone, swallowed up by the Ligurian sea, but took comfort in the knowledge that it was what she had wished, to be scattered about here in her little piece of paradise, Portovenere.

'Farewell, mother.' I whispered, sadness clasping my throat. 'God rest her soul,' replied Maria again blessing herself while Piero with eyes downcast removed his battered cap in reverence.

Our mission accomplished, the conversation turned to the wake which had been organised tonight. I had thought of having some sort of function at the cottage, perhaps a few drinks and nibbles, but Maria told me her friend Lucio who was on the Council had organised the wake be held in the ruins of Doria castle. Many of the villagers had been invited as word had circulated about the English girl and her mother who had visited here all those years ago. I had walked one morning to see the castle which proudly stands in a strategic viewpoint high above the waves, the gulf and the church. It was rather an arduous uphill walk but had been worth the effort as the view had been sublime. En route, I thought I had probably walked in mother's footsteps as she would surely have visited this place.

'Georgia,' said Maria. 'Come with me and I will introduce you to Lucio.'

Under a waxing moon, mother's wake had commenced. Among the ruins, trestle tables were replete with plates of salads, marinated fish, cold meats, cheeses and olives. Holding our glasses, Maria and I made our way through a group of villagers who, by the sound of their laughter and banter, all seemed to be enjoying themselves. There were old people hunched on fold up chairs and, on the grass, were dotted blankets on which reclined young parents surrounded by their children. Everyone wanted to talk to me, and there were many questions about mother's time spent here in their village. Had she swum with any poets? Was she one of their girl friends? This said with a wink of the eye by one of the old fishermen who was a friend of Piero's and had the same brown leathery skin. It was a picnic atmosphere and seemed to be a cross between New Year's Eve and a birthday party and I wondered what mother would have made of it all. I hoped she would have approved.

'Lucio.' Said Maria.

He was in the process of pulling a cork from a bottle of chianti.

'This is Georgia', Edwina's daughter.'

He put down the bottle and extended his hand.

'Buonasera, Georgia. It is good to meet you, my condolences on your mother's passing. I hope everything meets with your approval.'

'Grazie, Lucio.' I replied, 'Yes, everything is wonderful and I'm sure mother would have thought so too. I cannot believe how many people are here,' I added.

'Ah yes, us Italians love to celebrate especially in a little village such as this. It is a chance for everyone to see each other and catch up on the latest news.'

'Well, I think it is a lovely tradition and thank you once again for permitting the use of the grounds.'

'No problem.' He replied.

'More wine?'

I gratefully permitted another top up then, excusing myself to both him and Maria, walked towards the edge of the cliff. I sat down. I wanted to be on my own for a while, away from the hubbub which seemed to be now discordant, intruding on my thoughts. As I listened to the waves crashing against the cliff below, I imagined mother here with friends, perhaps that infamous group from England, carousing, discussing the state of the nation, or perhaps reading or listening to poetry. I sipped my wine and stared out over the church to the gulf of poets and wondered if mother had sat on this very spot entranced by the view. There was so much I did not know nor understand but I was hopeful that my journey here would for better or worse, perhaps render me a solution to the enigma, the enigma which was my mother.

CHAPTER 4

1926

'It's just too tiresome,' Harriette announced blurry eyed from the tangle of sheets in which she and her boy friend had been ensconced.

'What is?' Asked Ernest who was in the process of doing up his tie and not making a very good job of it.

'The invitation I received yesterday. It does not mention who is giving the party. It just says to show up at the swimming baths next Tuesday and wear red and white.'

He gave up on the tie and proceeded to comb his hair instead. In the mirror he saw her reflection, her hair which had been recently cut into a shingle. He disliked this new hair cut which most of the women were having. He preferred long hair on girls, it was more feminine. Hair he could let down and run his fingers through.

'Well, old bean, if you want to go, just turn up.' He replied.

'Yes, I suppose I shall, but I still think it is rather improper to not put one's name on it. I'll bet it's Lady Ebsworth. I can imagine her doing something like that, keeping us all in the dark, and,' she added conspiratorially, 'I heard she has been named as the co-respondent in the Haversham's divorce.'

'I say, said Ernest changing the subject, his need for tidbits of gossip unwanted at this hour of the morning, 'Don't you think you had better get up. I thought you started at nine?' He resumed assembling his tie and this time succeeded in a somewhat reasonable Windsor knot.

'What, oh there's no rush. Barney is there to open up and there are not many customers before ten anyway,' she said stifling a yawn.

Harriette, only daughter of the Labour Minister Anthony and Mrs Eleanora Cavendish had a job in an antiquarian bookshop in Chelsea and, according to her parents, lived way beyond her means. Her mother constantly bewailed her daughter's hedonistic life, as she frequented all sorts of clubs drinking, smoking and partying until the early hours as though there was no tomorrow. She thought it was a mystery how she acquired the money to fund such a lifestyle. Her acquaintances' offspring all seemed to be the same and over luncheons and dinner parties there was much talk of the young ones' behaviour. 'Do you know,' said Eleanora's friend, Dorothy her face turning puce at this affront to her sense of propriety. 'I saw my Cedric going out the other night dressed like a woman! I mean, I ask you, what is the world coming to? It wasn't like this in our day I can tell you.' This statement was followed by nods of agreement and lots of tut tutting by the assemblage.

'Please yourself then, I'm off,' announced Ernest walking to the door, 'Toodle loo, thanks for the romp.' He departed the mansion flat and hurried to the tube en route buying a newspaper from the paper boy on the corner and arrived just in time to catch his train. He was a reporter for the Daily Mail in Fleet Street having worked his way up the rungs from a cadetship. His job covered anything of interest ranging from accidents to society dos. The latter he enjoyed the most as it was at these functions, and as a member of the press, food and drink was always freely available. He enjoyed his job, the camaraderie in the office, the smell and noise of the printing presses churning out the reports he had written. When he was a cadet, it had taken him a while to become used to reporting on serious incidents but now he found he was a bit more desensitised to the foibles of human nature and took things in his stride. He settled himself into a seat and opened the paper but found he could not concentrate. He was in a quandary. He was undecided whether to continue seeing Harriette or pursue someone else like that girl with whom he had flirted at that soiree in the American bar last week. She was certainly a looker and judging from her attire was well heeled. Harrriette, at the moment was bleeding him dry. Lately he was giving her money to tide her over until she was paid. However, it was always, 'Oh, you know I am good for it Ernie' in that simpering voice of hers every time he had asked her for his money. He could not fathom how much she spent especially on clothes. 'But I have nothing to wear' would be her usual refrain as dresses and jackets were cast from the wardrobe ending up in a pile on the floor. He had the feeling she was using him and also had a suspicion she was seeing someone else. This suspicion had lain in the foothills of his mind and had surfaced when he had witnessed her with another woman a few weeks ago. He was reporting an incident at Euston station one Friday afternoon where a man had gone under a train. As he was receiving the details from the policeman, he witnessed Harriette and a woman boarding The Flying Scotsman bound for Scotland. She had told him she was going to spend the weekend visiting her grandmother who lived in Brighton. He recognised the woman as he had seen her a few weeks ago locked together with Harriette on the dance floor at the Blues Jazz Club in Piccadilly. It did not perturb him that she was dallying with a woman. At the moment, half the population were switching teams. Well, he decided, as the train glided into Blackfriars, good riddance to her. He tucked the unread paper into his pocket and prepared to alight.

'Morning, have a good night?' Jim asked as Ernest settled at his desk. Jim was one of the other reporters who covered the sports and was always ready to pass on any hot racing tips which came across his desk.

'Not bad.' Replied Ernest. He lit a cigarette, removed the cover from his typewriter and inserted some paper. He was always reticent to discuss personal matters in the office especially his dalliances. He changed the subject.

'Goodwood is on today, isn't it? Got any tips?'

'Ah, funny you should ask old chum. As a matter of fact, my sources say put your shirt on number five in the seventh. A nag called Who Shot the Barman. Apparently, it's going to romp home.'

'What are the odds?'

'About twenty to one I think.'

Ernest wrote down the name of the horse and thought he would wager a few pounds on it. He would do an each way bet so he would at least win something if it got a place. He certainly could do with a win at the moment.

'I can put the bets on at the track,' said Jim noticing his colleague pulling some notes from his wallet. 'The odds are better at the course.'

'Put twenty each way,' said Ernest handing over the pounds.

'The last of the big spenders, eh?' Quipped Jim as he folded up the notes and stuffed them into his pocket.

'Something like that,' answered Ernest. 'Let's hope you didn't get put onto a bum steer like that other hot tip you gave me last month. That nag is still running!'

The telephone rang.

'Daily Mail.' Announced Ernest.

He took the pencil from behind his ear and jotted down some notes on his pad.

'Righto, thanks. I will be right there.'

'Got a job?' Asked Jim who had turned his attention to making a cup of tea. The office had decided to purchase an electric jug for the convenience of the staff and Jim had been making full use of it.

'There's some sort of disturbance at Oxford Circus.'

'Better get your skates on.'

'See you later then. Don't forget about the bets,' Ernest threw over his shoulder on the way out.

He hailed a taxi as it was faster than taking the train. The paper always recompensed their staff for transport expenses as they needed their reporters to be the first on the scene to get the scoop.

'Where to Guv?'

'Oxford Circus and please hurry.'

'Right you are.'

They sped off past the old bank of England, and along Bond Street where they became ensnared in a traffic jam.

'Sorry Guv. This doesn't look good.'

There was nothing for it but to wait it out as all the vehicles were moving at a snail's pace.

Ernest decided he would not stress about the situation. He would not be the only reporter caught up so decided to ignore the toots of the cars and settle back in his seat. He looked through the window at the people going about their activities; business men in pin stripe suits, mothers pushing prams, and women, their shingled hair adorned by cloche hats. He wondered what had happened at Oxford Circus and hoped no one had been injured or killed. He remembered what it had been like only a couple of months ago in May, when the great strike had occurred. Then there were huge traffic jams as bus and train drivers ceased working along with hundreds of others who supported the coal miners. They had been locked out by the owners who wanted them to work longer hours for less money. Fights had broken out and people had been hit by the police with batons. Ernest had been laid off for nine days as the publishing industry had also shut down in solidarity. The strike had resonated greatly with Ernest, as his father worked at the Tyldesley colliery in Manchester. He endured a hard life underground digging in the dark and breathing in the coal dust which settled on the lungs and, more often than not, resulting in an early demise. However, his father had not known anything else, following his father before him descending into the bowels of the earth in the coal pits of Wales. He had told Ernest many times that there was a great camaraderie in the mines, everyone being there for each other through the good times and the bad. During the strike Ernest had visited his father. He had been offered a lift by an acquaintance whose uncle was also a miner at the Tyldesley colliery and was as keen as Ernest to visit and offer some succour. During the five hour journey he was concerned about the sort of welcome he would receive. His father had always been a proud man and did not take kindly to handouts. Any money offered by his son would be strongly refused, so he had bought some food for the family and given it to his mother who, with tears in her eyes, took it with no objection. She knew they had to have food to sustain them through the strike the duration of which was unknown. His father had railed a bit initially but Ernest had made him see sense. 'If you don't want food for yourself Dad, that is fair enough.' Ernest exhorted. 'But you cannot deny Mum and Herbie.' His father had wrung his hands and looked over at the wan face of his youngest son, the son handicapped since birth, unable to work, sitting in a wheelchair. 'No, you're right, son.' He said shaking his head, his shoulders heaving. 'I cannot let my family starve.' Then, regaining composure, he stood up and exclaimed, 'Mother, what are you waiting for? Get these potatoes on to boil so we can have our tea.'

Ernest had stayed three nights with his family in the tiny miner's cottage. Sleeping on the small sofa beside the cooking range his ears were attuned to every noise, the snuffling of Herbie, the creaking of the wood but the worst was his father's coughing. He had always feared his father's health would suffer in the mines and was glad that he had been fortunate to have received an education, a pass out of this existence, and into a job in a London office.

During his stay with his family, he ventured to the shops bringing back more supplies to tide them over. On the fourth day he departed for London and, as the kitchen reverberated with teary farewells, he managed to stuff some pounds into his mother's apron pocket. The strike had lasted a total of nine days and, ten days after that, his father had been diagnosed with the Black Lung disease, the disease which along with other miners had ultimately claimed his father in Wales.

The taxi was now on the move and Oxford Circus was in sight.

'Thanks, driver,' said Ernest. 'You can let me out here. I can walk the rest of the way.'

'Right you are then Guv.'

Ernest paid the driver and commenced walking. Up ahead he could see some people milling about and there was an ambulance and a police car. Ernest approached the sergeant who was on the fringe of the crowd among which were reporters and photographers who like Ernest jostled to obtain information.

'What happened?' He asked producing his Press Card.

'Domestic dispute' replied the officer.

Ernest took out his notebook and pencil and commenced jotting down the details: Man assaults wife's lover on his way to work. Injuries sustained; a broken nose, bruising and facial lacerations, assailant taken into police custody.

'Thanks officer, that's about all I need,' said Ernest putting away his notebook. 'Have a good day.' He added as the throng dispersed and the camera men scampered off to their dark rooms.

He walked to the nearest telephone box to ring the office with his report and to ask if there was anything else he had to cover before he went to the luncheon at the Ritz. He dialled the number but received an engaged tone. He hung up and dialled again. It felt hot standing in the box. The sun was beating in through the window. He loosened his tie, the line was still engaged. Well, he was not going to stand here all day. Time was ticking on and he had to be at the luncheon by 11.30. Although it would usually take a taxi about ten minutes to get there if the traffic was as bad as it had been this morning he might be late. He gave the office one last try and then gave up. If there was something to be covered someone else would have to do it, like that fellow who had just commenced as a cadet. He had to learn the ropes and the only way was to jump in and do it and the sooner the better. That is what he had done, jumping in at the deep end. His first report had been a traffic accident where a woman had gone under a bus. It had been a terrible scene to witness and even now, years later, he still had visions of the poor soul's mangled bloody legs as they tried to free her. Abandoning his thoughts to the telephone box, he hailed a taxi and arrived at the Ritz in plenty of time to survey the milieu before the throng descended.

CHAPTER 5

1985

The day after the wake I had caught a chill leading to a chest infection so my plan of looking through mother's box had come to nought. I spent nearly a week in bed being ministered to by Maria who dropped by the cottage every day bringing home-made chicken soup and other delicacies to tempt my flagging appetite. She even summoned the doctor who prescribed antibiotics and ordered me to stay in bed. Piero had also visited and decided he would move the television into my bedroom 'So signora will not be bored.' He had said. I did not have the heart to tell him that everything on the television was in Italian and nearly impossible for me to comprehend. The whole village seemed to be aware of my plight as, every day, Maria brought with her their get- well messages. As I lay in my bed, I pondered how lovely were these Portovenerians who had befriended me and taken me into their hearts.

After I had recovered sufficiently and when the weather was fine, I took my books and sat outside in the garden as I still was not in the mood to sort through the box As I felt the warmth of the sun on my face it felt as though I had been released from prison. I loved being outdoors and had hated being cooped up inside for a week especially in bed feeling unwell. Piero and Maria continued to drop by, Maria ensuring I was eating nourishing food, food which she bought for me so I would not have to venture to the shops. I felt grateful for her help as I knew she was busy at home looking after Marko and Piero who lived with them. Also, as a seamstress she was occupied filling orders for dresses which she had made. She had told me that she had inherited the love of sewing from her mother, making lace in the Venetian village of Burano until she died last year at the age of ninety eight. I had visited this unique village and had been entranced by the houses all painted brightly in different colours, while the front doors festooned with curtains fluttered in the breeze. Piero continued to busy himself in the garden, darting around picking up stray leaves and fallen twigs and watering the plants. He always called me Signora, never my first name. I supposed it was because he was of that generation who tended to be more formal and had respect for women and I found I quite liked this form of address.

I had now recovered from my illness and felt well enough to have Maria over for lunch. I thought it was a way of repaying her for her kindness and also to reciprocate for the dinners I had consumed at her house. It would be also an opportunity for the two of us to discuss things without the presence of the men, a woman to woman talk. I wanted to tell her about mother, and ask her if anything more had surfaced in her father's memory about the time when she was here.

We were to lunch alfresco. I had set up a table and chairs in a sheltered spot in the garden away from any cool breezes which may decide to spring up from the gulf. I was just pouring the olive oil and vinegar over the tomato and basil when I noticed through the window Maria approaching.

'Buongiorno.' I said throwing open the door.

She kissed me on both cheeks and thrust a bottle of prosecco into my hands

'Oh, Maria, thank you. But you should not have brought anything.' I said as I gratefully took the wine.

'Nonsense, Georgia,' she replied. 'I cannot come to lunch without bringing something.'

'Well, it is lovely of you.'

'Do you need any help?' She offered looking at the salad I had made.

'No, everything is ready. I thought we would eat in the garden as it is such a nice day,' I added as I finished pouring the dressing over the salad.

Maria agreed and we carried out the plates of cold chicken and ham, the baguettes and the salad.

'To us,' Maria exclaimed as we clinked our glasses.

It was lovely sitting here in the warmth of the garden breaking bread with my friend and I momentarily thought of mother. Had she also sat out here with a friend enjoying an alfresco meal laughing and talking just as Maria and I were now doing?

'A penny for your thoughts.' Quipped Maria noticing my preoccupation.

'Oh, sorry Maria, I was just thinking if my mother used to have lunch out here with a friend.'

'I think she probably would have.' She replied, swotting away a fly which was attempting to land on a slice of tomato. 'You must have been close to your mother coming all the way over here to scatter her ashes.'

I took a good sip of wine.

'As a matter of fact, we weren't close at all. It has been only recently before her death that I reconciled with her and agreed to stay here in the cottage.'

It was after that explanation and over more wine (a second bottle had been opened) I found myself confiding in Maria. I told her all about my childhood, my mother's moods and incapacity to show affection towards my father. I told her about the box of photos I had brought with me and my intention to learn whatever I could about my mother's earlier life. She had sat listening intently to every word and it was when I had stopped talking that her eyes had filled with tears. I did not think my story would have had such an effect on her and I reached over to pat her hand.

She withdrew a tissue from her pocket and blew her nose.

'Sorry, Georgia, I did not mean to be upset.'

'It's ok. I should probably not have told you all that but I think I needed to get it off my chest.'

'That is right, sometimes these things we need to talk about.' She worried the beads at her neck. I noticed they were made of the glass from Murano, the next village on from where her grandmother had lived.

'However', she continued. 'It was not so much what you told me which made me upset.'

'Oh, wasn't it?' I queried as I poured us more wine.

'No,' she replied now more composed. 'It was you talking about your mother that made me think of what happened to me.'

'Do you want to tell me about it?' I ventured.

'I don't know. It is not something I have told to many people.'

I looked across at her and had the feeling she wanted to tell me. She and I seemed to have developed a rapport in the short time I had spent here. We felt comfortable with each other and, as she had said, sometimes things are better shared with someone else.

As an emerging grey cloud threw the garden into shadow, Maria recounted her story and I felt somewhat comforted by the fact that I was not the only one whose childhood had also been impaired.

CHAPTER 6

1926

Ernest shouldered his way through the lunchtime carousal of the Stab in the Back and headed straight to the bar where he ordered a ploughman's lunch and a pint of bitter. As he waited, he kept his eye out for Jim and a few of the other journalists who were to join him. He knew it would be a long lunch as it was Friday, the day when all staff from the Fourth Estate filled the pubs to overflowing. Fleet Street was one great watering hole which, if you walked fast enough, could be traversed during the rain without getting wet. The Stab was Ernest's favourite drinking place. It was less packed and more casual than El Vino where jackets were always insisted upon, or the Old Press Club in Salisbury Court where the leather and polished wood reminded him of a staid old Gentlemen's Club. He took a swig of his beer then glanced at his watch. They were ten minutes late. He hoped they had not decided to go with Jim to the White Swan the pub of choice for sports' editors. He was nibbling on a pickle when he felt a slap on his shoulder.

'What's doing chum?' Announced Jim 'Sorry to be late, had to finish that football article for tomorrow's edition.'

Ernest turned around to face him.

'I thought you might have gone to the Swan.' He said. 'Where are the others?'

'They decided to go the Tavern instead. I think it was something to do with the fairer sex. What are you drinking?'

'Bitter,' said Ernest now assembling some ham and cheese onto the bread.

Jim placed the same order as his colleague.

'Well, another Friday comes around,' said Jim settling back in his chair.

'Yes, that it does.' Agreed Ernest taking a bite of his sandwich.

The barman placed Jim's bitter before him and their glasses were raised in a toast to a busy week and the win they had at the races. Jim's tip had paid off as Who Shot the Barman had romped home at twenty to one.

'Anything exciting planned for the weekend?' Asked Jim.

'Not sure yet, might have a quiet one for a change.'

'Oh, I thought you would be painting the town red with your winnings.'

Ernest bit into another pickle. He should be doing exactly that. Out on the town with a pretty woman in tow, not sitting in his flat reading novels or listening to dance music on the wireless. He would usually be spending Saturday night with Harriette but he had soon severed that relationship, cutting short her wheedling phone calls as the image of her and that woman remained uppermost in his mind. He regretted not obtaining a contact number for that good sort with whom he had flirted at the American.

'Dulcie and I are going to the Ambassador tomorrow night.' Announced Jim. 'There's a good band playing. You would be welcome to join us if you're at a loose end.'

Dulcie who was Jim's wife of thirty years enjoyed tripping the light fantastic, a beer and a day at the races, the latter sometimes attended with Jim when he had a fixture to cover.

Ernest took a swig of beer.

'Ok thanks, I'll think about it.'

He added. 'Sounds like you will be kicking up your heels. How much did you win on that nag if you don't mind my asking?'

Jim lit a cigarette, inhaled and blew a curl of smoke into the air.

'Ha, we cleaned up. Dulcie had fifty on the nose and I had a hundred.'

'Blimey,' exclaimed Ernest. 'As much as that. Well, make sure you put some away for that rainy day. You never know what's ahead. I've heard a few rumblings around the traps that we might be in for a downturn. Apparently, people aren't spending like they used to, not as many cars being bought either.'

'Thanks for the tip, I'll be sensible.' Replied Jim whose upper lip was now sporting an amount of white beer foam.

The afternoon sloshed around in copious libations. Their colleagues having decided the Tavern was not to their liking decided to join them and there was much discussion about the economy and various other topics. Around five o'clock they, and the rest of the Fleet Street contingent, piled into the waiting taxis to be disgorged at their respective addresses.

'Don't forget,' Jim yelled through the window as Ernest stumbled out onto the footpath.

'Ambassadish!'

Ernest gave the thumbs up. He staggered to the door of his flat and finding his key let himself in. He awoke on the sofa a few hours later with a raging thirst, a splitting headache and the usual vow never again to spend all Friday afternoon in the pub.

As Ernest lay inebriated on the sofa, Harriette along with a few of the Mayfair set was in a taxi en route to another night of merriment in Notting Hill.

'I say,' announced Cyril 'Does anyone know the address of this place?'

'It's supposed to be in Ledbury Road,' piped up Harriette.

'What number in Ledbury Road?'

'Oh, I don't know Cyril, I think they said there will be a flag outside.'

'A flag?' queried Priscilla. 'Are we supposed to walk the length of the street until we see a flag?'

'Quite right darl' I'm blowed if I am walking around half the night. These shoes are killing me. I don't know how you women put up with it.' This from Edward who was wearing a pair of high heels and garbed in an above the knee black lace gown.

'It's not far from here,' exclaimed Harriette peering through the window as the taxi approached Westbourne Grove.

'We shall get out now, thank you driver,' she said.

Cyril paid the fare, they poured out of the taxi then peered at the townhouses hoping to see any indication of a flag.

'I've an idea,' said Harriette. 'Cill and I will go up one end of the street and Cyril and Edward do the other. Whoever sees the flag will call out.'

Just as there was about to be dissension in the ranks, from around the corner a group of party goers appeared the leader of which held aloft the Union Jack.

'I say,' said Cyril. 'Let's follow them. They look like they are going to the same soiree. What jolly luck.'

They commenced following the merry makers who, by the sound of their caterwauling, appeared to have already made an early start on liquid refreshments.

'I thought the bloody flag was supposed to be already on the house.' Commented Edward tottering along, his shoes threatening to upend him into the gutter. Nobody paid him any attention, they being used to his usual petulance.

Priscilla and Harriette walked together albeit at a distance. Since the weekend spent in Scotland they had been seeing each other sporadically. As well as the altercation in which Priscilla had accused her lover of flirting with another woman, Harriette's fickleness ran close to the surface. She seemed to tire easily of her conquests, discarding them and moving on to the next new thing on the scene. Her proclivity was mainly towards women although the dalliance she had with Ernest had been more or less satisfying, which was more than could be said for some of the others. Perhaps it had something to do with the money he had given her, helping her out of tight squeezes. Poor old Ernest, he was rather a pushover and too trusting for his own good.

Arriving at the townhouse they trooped through a motley crowd, the air already pungent with cigarette and cigar smoke. From a gramophone in the corner of the room the strains of Duke Ellington competed with the popping of champagne corks and raucous laughter.

'Ooh, darling,' exclaimed a red lipped siren approaching Edward in a short black shimmy dress. 'Love the ensemble.'

Edward did an unsteady twirl nearly falling over.

'Woopsie.'

'And I haven't had a drink yet either,' he joked.

'We will soon fix that.' She grabbed a bottle of champagne from a nearby table and poured a generous measure into glasses.

'There we are then, cheers.'

'Oh, yes, Liz, bottoms up and all that,' answered Edward.

'I think I might sit down'. He added. 'These shoes are rather rough on the old feet. As I said to the gang on the way here, I don't know how you women put up with them.'

'Oh, we learn to get used to it.' Replied Liz. 'But your idea is a good one Eddy. Let's sit down and you can let me know all the goss. I haven't seen you for about three weeks.'

They squashed onto a sofa on which sat a couple in the throes of intimacy. Ignoring their ardour Liz lit a cigarette sat back, turned to Edward and said. 'Ok, Eddy what's been happening?'

He took a good swallow of the champagne.

'Well, darl.' He commenced. 'Looks like Harriette has flicked off Ernest or maybe it is the other way around.'

'I thought as much when I saw her tonight. 'It's rather sick making,' replied Liz. 'I wonder how long this one will last?'

'Who would know,' he replied. 'She changes partners as fast as a bride's nightie comes off.'

'Ha, that's good,' she said mirthfully poking him in the ribs.

'How long have they been an item?' Enquired Liz inclining her gaze towards Harriette and Priscilla who were now on the floor giving a rather desultory rendition of the Charleston.

'Only about a month or so, although I think there will soon be a parting of the ways. They spent a weekend at Davenport's pile in Perthshire and Priscilla did a bolt rather early. Old Harry was up to her usual tricks,' 'And' he added conspiratorially, 'She had told Ernest she was visiting her ailing grandmother in Brighton.'

'Oh, what a situation, she is rather a beast.' Replied Liz. 'It seems as though they are all better off without her.' She took another puff of her cigarette 'I don't know why she kept on with Ernest when she doesn't really prefer the male species.'

'Yes, quite right, darl. He leaned over and whispered. 'Methinks he was her financier. By what I hear he used to lend her money all the time.'

Liz manifested a moue at this comment as she had been unaware just how devious Harriette was.

'Well, I can't imagine this one will be throwing any funds her way,' she said her eyes scrutinising Priscilla. 'The jewellery she is wearing does not look like it would be worth much' 'And,' she added. 'She does look rather young.'

'Yes, my thoughts exactly,' replied Edward.

'I pity her,' said Liz. 'Harriette can be quite dictatorial.'

'Quite,' said Edward. 'Maybe she was grooming her to be her little protégé.'

Liz fondled her pearls.

'Do you know where they met?'

'Oh, I think Cyril said it was at an art exhibition at one of the small galleries. Apparently Cill's friend was the artist.' Replied Edward.

'Oh, do you know his name?'

'I think it was Stevens or Stephenson, something like that.'

'Doesn't ring a bell. 'However,' she added. 'He must be someone up and coming. Harriette would not have bothered to attend otherwise.'

'No, darl, quite right. She does like to lean towards anyone of note.'

He put down his glass and hoisted himself from the sofa.

'But enough of her,' he suddenly announced taking Liz's hand.

'How about we show them all how the Charleston should be done?'

Liz put down her glass, Edward abandoned his shoes and they joined the other couples gyrating to the music.

The night drifted on as more people arrived and it was after 1.00am when Harriette announced that she and Priscilla were repairing to a Club where the jazz was smooth and the people smoother. Cyril and Edward declined; Cyril because he had to attend a court case in the morning, he being the solicitor for the defence, and Edward because his feet were now in such a state he thought that only a soak in Epsom salts would restore them to some sort of normalcy.

A cab deposited the two women outside a smoky den in Soho. It was one of Harriette's favourite places where, among other things, one was not censured for indulging in cocaine. Lately it was becoming rather an addiction and she found she was requiring more and more money to fund it.

Through the fug she located a table in the corner.

'That was fortunate,' she said settling herself.

'What shall we drink?' Timorously asked Priscilla.

'Oh, I should think a brandy at this hour.' Replied Harriette waving to a waiter who hurried over to take their order.

'Two brandies my good man,' she commanded.

'Oh,' said Priscilla hesitantly. 'I was rather thinking of having something else.'

The waiter hovered while Priscilla tried to make up her mind.

'Just have a brandy, Cill. I should think you have had enough of the bubbly tonight.'

'Ok then, a brandy,' she acquiesced.

The waiter nodded and returned to the bar.

Harriette opened her evening purse and withdrew her snuff box. She opened it and took a snort of the white powder within.

'Want some?' She asked Priscilla.

'Me? Oh no, thank you. I will stick to the brandy.'

'You should live a little,' said Harriette 'You are always so strait laced.'

The brandies arrived. Priscilla took a sip. She really had not wanted brandy but Harriette had forced her into having one. She seemed to be always making her do things, she was beginning to feel dominated but felt rather powerless to ameliorate the situation.

Suddenly Harriette grabbed her arm and attempted to pull her off the chair as a black singer's mellifluous tones filled the room.

'Let's dance!' she exclaimed.

'What?' Oh, I really don't want to. I would rather sit here and finish my drink.'

'Spoilsport,' she spat releasing her grip then threaded her way uncertainly through the lamp lit tables where she disported herself directly in front of the startled singer. It was when she had grabbed the microphone Priscilla decided she had had enough. She left her companion and her half finished brandy and hurried from the club. On her way home in a cab she was unsure if she had done the right thing. Maybe she should have gone to Harriette's aid and not bolted like a skittish horse. But she knew what Harriette's reaction would have been. She was a solipsist, too intransigent and would not have accepted her aid or anyone else's. She should not have come. She should have stood her ground and refused but it was rather difficult where Harriette was concerned, she was always so persuasive and manipulative drawing her in when she felt vulnerable. She should have learnt her lesson in Scotland. It had started well enough. The two of them ensconced in a first-class sleeper as the Flying Scotsman steamed its way through the highlands to Perthshire, Priscilla thinking how sophisticated it was to be accompanying Harriette for a weekend at Henley Hall. She still lived in Ealing with her middle-class parents, they remaining completely oblivious to their daughter's lesbian tendencies.

With its mullioned windows, crenelated roof and liveried servants the Hall certainly had lived up to Priscilla's expectations. They had been shown to their room by the obsequious butler followed by a footman who had carried their suitcases up two flights of stairs, the scent of beeswax and lilies heavy in the air. A maid had then appeared and set about unpacking their suitcases. Priscilla had not expected this. She had thought she would be putting away her clothes especially her chain store underwear which was in dire need of replacing. Up until now she had managed not to let Harriette see them. Her underwear was of the highest quality, French lacy knickers and the finest silk stockings which she commanded her lovers to peel off prior to any sexual activity.

'I certainly hope you have something decent to wear to dinner tonight.' Admonished Harriette, her eyes alighting on a pair of dowdy knickers the maid was now folding into the drawer 'This underwear really is beyond the pale.' Suffused with embarrassment in front of the maid, Priscilla thought of the green dress she had planned to wear. It was not new but she was under the impression it suited her well enough at least that was what her mother had told her the last time she had worn it. 'It looks very nice on you Cill. It suits your dark hair.' Said her mother knitting needles clicking. Her father had looked up from behind his paper 'Your mother is right, pet. The dress does suit you.' However, judging by Harriette's view of her underwear she knew her dress would be entirely unsuitable. This had proved the case as, prior to and throughout the dinner, Harriette had all but ignored her. Over canapés in the library, Harriette had waxed lyrical among the other guests one of which was a woman who had sat opposite Harriette at dinner. Over the pheasant they had sought each other out engaging in banter and repartee leaving Priscilla to talk to the elderly Lord Salisbury who was hard of hearing. The evening had ended in tears and recriminations as Priscilla emboldened by alcohol accused her lover of abandonment and humiliation.

'Oh, come now, Cill, you are making too much of it. I was only having a little fun.'

'Fun?' Priscilla screamed. 'Fun? 'You call that fun? You ignored and humiliated me and you flirted outrageously with that woman. Everyone noticed.'

'Shoosh, everybody will hear you if you don't stop it. I have a reputation to uphold.'

'Reputation? It's all you think about isn't it, your precious reputation. What about considering other people's feelings for once? You left me battling on my own. You said you would look after me. You know how I am with company, especially in a place like this. Oh, I wish I had not come.' She sobbed flinging herself onto the bed.

'Oh, for goodness sake', Harriette retorted. 'Stop the hysterics, blubbing like a baby. It's about time you grew up. We will talk in the morning when you have calmed down.'

Ignoring Priscilla's distress, she sauntered over to the dressing table and, from her evening bag, withdrew a ring which she had pilfered from Salisbury's room. She had crept into the bedroom when the guests were assembled in the library for pre-dinner drinks. She thought the ring would not be missed as she had quite a collection and, judging by the old girl's behaviour at dinner, senility was coming to the fore. If it was missed the blame would be put on one of the staff who had the reputation of being light fingered. Nobody would ever consider she was the thief. As Priscilla had intimated, her reputation was beyond reproach and, like her parents, especially her father the Hon Anthony Cavendish, she had been gracing the main house on many occasions. She turned the ring over and scrutinised it carefully. It appeared to be a Columbian emerald and would procure a good price on the black market enabling her addiction. Now she had finished with Ernest there was nobody to whom she could turn for a loan. Satisfied, she tucked the ring back into the bag then withdrew the snuff box containing her supply. She inhaled deeply then retreated to a place where the sounds and feelings of her lover failed to discomfit her.

CHAPTER 7

1985

The summer heat having diminished and with my health regained, I was hiking to Manarola another of the Cinque Terre villages which clung to the cliffs. Since Maria had confided in me she and I had bonded more closely. It took courage for her to tell me that the woman whom she thought to be her mother, who had raised and nurtured her since babyhood, had actually been her aunt. Last year as she lay dying, her aunt had told Maria the tragic story that a priest had raped her mother resulting in Maria's conception. She had been whisked off to a convent in Murano away from village gossip and the shame. Maria's aunt had pretended to be pregnant and when the baby was born she had slipped away to the convent, returning with the baby and raising her as her own child. She had also been told that her mother had died while giving birth to Maria and her grave was in the cemetery at the back of the convent.

As I enfolded her into my arms trying to allay her distress, I thought of our similar experiences, both being told things by the dying breaths of our mothers. After Maria calmed, she said she possessed ambivalent feelings about the momentous news. She had only known her aunt as her mother, the woman who nurtured and raised her to be the person she now was. However, she felt a terrible loss and sadness for her real mother, exiled in secrecy, giving birth in a convent and dying there away from the family she had known and loved.

Picking my way along the Manarola trail beside which grew a plethora of cacti and other indeterminate flowers endemic to the area, I noticed the cliff draped with the ruins of the tiny terraced vineyards. My thoughts turned to Maria and I hoped her life would not also be reduced to ruins. If her aunt had said nothing Maria would not have been any the wiser. Now, her life was turned upside down and all because a dying woman did not want to go to her grave with a secret. What of my life? Would I discover something about my mother which would have a deleterious effect on me?

I had looked through the box one morning but there did not seem to be anything much of interest apart from two faded sepia photos. One was of my parents and a woman sitting on a rug in a meadow, a picnic basket beside them. The other was of mother and this other woman sunbathing on a rock. My interest had been somewhat piqued as I turned it over and noticed there was scrawled PV July 1928. Could PV stand for Portovenere? The back of the other photo in which father had featured had been left blank. By the way they were all cosied up to one another, I assumed they were quite good friends. The woman had a retrousse nose and blonde shingled hair whereas mother's hair was longer and dark. Father garbed in breeches had brought a smile to my face as through the years I had nearly always seen him in a suit and tie. I had approached Piero and asked him if he had recognised these people especially the woman but his mind was again blank. However, he told me that there might be someone in the next village, in Manarola, someone who might be able to help me in my quest. I did not hold out much hope. Whoever it was might well by now be deceased but still it was worth a try so with the photos secured in my backpack I pushed on.

The village was rising from its morning torpor. The locals were out with their baskets and the cafes were setting up for lunch. I thought before attempting to locate the address Piero had given me I would firstly find somewhere to eat. I walked along the caruggi and soon settled on a tiny cafe which had alfresco dining. It suited me perfectly and, my appetite whetted by the walk, I soon devoured one of the specialties of the area, a soufflé di scampi pie. With a glass of limone, I sat back and absorbed the village scene. With its jumble of houses festooned with washing fluttering in the breeze, it was similar to Portovenere. Black garbed grandmothers engrossed in conversation sat on the front steps, while outside the bars mopish young males loitered, espresso in one hand and cigarette in the other. One of them glanced in my direction and I returned his gaze. With his hair flopping over his eyes, he reminded me of Peter with whom I had the first serious relationship after my enrolment at university. After we had been out a few times he had become rather smitten and had wanted more than I could offer. I seemed to crave more the company of women, of which he had been made aware prior to the severance of our friendship. He had discovered me and another girl in a rather compromising position on a lounge at a party. I thought I felt this way because of my experiences at boarding school where there would be playful fondling under the sheets when lights were extinguished. Then it had been like a game one played and I knew it also occurred at boys' schools as well. It was something akin to a rite of passage through which one travelled however, the feelings persisted along with confusion about my sexuality. I am still trying to come to terms with it and had been unable to discuss it with mother. The first time I had tremulously broached the subject her eyebrows had risen briefly with some understanding before sinking down with confused anxiety. She had returned to her task in hand, casting around for another subject to discuss.

After paying the bill and obtaining directions from the waiter, I set off to find Giovanna Donato, the lady who Piero had said might be able to recognise the people in the photo. She had lived around the area and had spent time in Portovenere around the same time as mother and her ilk. As I walked further away from the cafe the streets twisted and turned and I noticed that I was walking in the direction of the church of San Lorenzo. I determined to visit it after seeing Signora Donato. I continued on and, apart from a couple of stray mangy looking cats, there did not appear to be anyone about and my fear of becoming lost began to increase. I had been once lost in the Lake District. I was staying at a hotel and had ventured for a walk into the next village. One of the staff had advised me to take a short cut through the gardens so I had set off across the grass and along a track through some bushland eventually arriving at a road which took me to the village. I had enjoyed a few hours exploring the shops of Windermere and having lunch. When it was time to return to the hotel, I had retraced my steps along the road but could not locate the bush track from which I had exited. There were many places along the road all looking similar but I could not find the correct one. I walked along other roads and other tracks even at one stage thinking I had located my hotel, similar as it was to mine but no avail. One of the staff directed me as to where I should walk but still I could not locate it. I knocked on someone's door in the hope that they would know where my hotel was but even they could not direct me. I thought of summoning a taxi but there was nary one to be seen. However just as I was thinking I would never find the place, I encountered a young girl walking along the road and she knew exactly where I had to walk. I had been so grateful when I eventually arrived. Sweaty and dishevelled I had made my way to the bathroom to freshen up before ordering a large gin and tonic in the lounge to calm my shattered nerves. Now I had that same feeling but just as I thought of knocking on one of the doors to ask directions, I turned a corner and there was the house with the blue door, the door behind which hopefully would be Signora Donato who could assist in my endeavour. I knocked and waited, then knocked again. Obviously there was no one home. I turned to walk away when the door opened.

'Si?' asked the diminutive presence a puzzled look on her face.

'Oh, boungiorno' I said, 'Signora Donato?'

'Non, non Donato.'

I quickly withdrew my Italian phrase book from my backpack and looked up some words as this lady could not speak English.

'Allora.' I replied. 'Sai dove e?' 'Do you know where she is'?

'Signora in Casa di Riposo.'

A nursing home is what she was telling me.

'Grazie, dove?' I asked. 'Where is it?'

'Monterosso.' She replied making the sign of the cross as she did so.

I thanked her for her help and she closed the door on my disappointment. If my source was in a nursing home I was not optimistic of retrieving any information. The poor lady was bound to be in a frail condition and could even be suffering from dementia or some other ailment peculiar to old age. I put away the phrase book and then decided to venture to the church in the hope it would not take too much time to locate it. I commenced walking and as I ascended a steep incline the spire of the church hove into view. Inside all was quiet apart from an elderly man kneeling in prayer and a woman placing a lighted candle into one of the sconces. Genuflecting before the altar, I took a seat in one of the pews and perceived the smell which always seemed to permeate old churches; cold stale air and candle wax. When I had visited San Pietro church my senses had not been attuned to anything much other than mother's ashes and their ultimate disposal.

Sitting there, my eyes were drawn to the rose window at the back of the altar. It reminded me of the one which had been in the church to which my father would take me when I was a child, the church of St Mary's at Thorpeness. Every Sunday morning he would take me to mass as mother kept to her bed, she not interested in any form of religion. 'What sort of god is it who would inflict so much suffering on the world?' She would murmur apropos of nobody whenever we set off for church. My father seemed to draw great comfort and peace from his religion especially on Sundays. Although this day of the week tended to be rather boring for me as there was nothing much open, at least the atmosphere at home was peaceful. Maybe it was because mother had some time to herself when we were at church busying herself in the kitchen and roasting the lamb whose aromas greeted us upon our return. Cooking seemed to be one of the few things mother enjoyed especially when there was a tart to be cooked or bread to be baked. Her frustrations would be taken out on the dough as it would be kneaded, slapped and rolled to within an inch of its life.

Glancing at my watch, I saw it was getting late and it would take me another hour to hike back to Portovenere. I prayed for my parents and Maria and for help in my quest then walked over to the side altar and lit a candle. Outside all was still quiet. I decided to return the way I had come, back to the cafe thence to the commencement of the track which would lead me back to Portovenere. Down and around the curuggi I walked, past the house at which I had knocked, past the cats which were now curled up asleep outside one of the houses. As I approached the cafe and the bar, I noticed they were deserted the customers having now absconded for the afternoon siesta. It reminded me how tired I was now feeling and I still had to walk for another hour. Maybe I should not have undertaken this hike so soon after my illness I mused. However, it was too late for recriminations. I would just have to persevere and look forward to a restful night's sleep upon my return. I was soon shaken from my reverie as I suddenly became aware of someone walking behind me.

Turning around, I discovered it was the floppy haired loiterer who I had noticed earlier outside the bar.

'Oh, Buongiorno,' I said as a friendly gesture.

'Putana, whore!' he suddenly screamed punching me in the face and throwing me to the ground. I landed on my back, the breath knocked out of me and felt the spines of the cacti pricking my arms. He dragged me off the track and into a clump of bushes and an instant later he was astride my waist pinning me to the ground.

I lashed out at him, hitting and scratching but my struggles to fend him off were proving worthless against his strength. Terrified, I could hardly process what was happening.

'Do, do you want money?' I tearfully offered in a desperate attempt at appeasement.

'Sta zito, shut up!' He yelled as his hand clamped on my mouth. As I felt my jeans being frenziedly ripped from my legs, I hoped and prayed that rape would be the worst ordeal I would have to endure. Anything else was too horrific to contemplate.

CHAPTER 8

1926

After Priscilla had left in high dudgeon early on the Sunday train to London, Harriette had wasted no time in resuming her friendship with the woman with whom she had flirted over dinner. She discovered that they seemed to be kindred spirits and Harriette relished the challenge of winning her over from the clutches of her male companion, a rather timorous solicitor at law. His company, Murphy & Dugdale, had acted for many years for Lord and Lady Salisbury drawing up and amending their wills and testaments and advising them on matters pertaining to the estate.

'Well, if you prefer to be addressed as Ed old bean, I rather prefer Harry,' announced Harriette as they sprawled together on a rug by the river. A picnic lunch had been organised, the footmen transporting baskets of food and wine together with other accoutrements down through the gardens from the Hall.

Ed lit a cigarette and sipped her champagne into which she had added a strawberry.

'Is your friend ill?' she asked. 'Only I did not see her at breakfast this morning.'

'Cill? Silly thing did a bolt and caught the early train back to London. She has these moods which I must say are getting rather too boring.'

'I see.' Replied Ed now waving to Tom who was currently rowing one of the dinghies. He returned her wave.

'Anything serious with the rower?' Asked Harriette looking in his direction.

She returned her gaze and fingered her brooch.

'Oh, Tom? We have been seeing each other for a while. He's keen to marry but I'm not so sure. I rather like to have a few options open if you know what I mean.'

Harriette kicked off her shoes and wiggled her toes.

'My thoughts exactly, one must explore and experience quite a deal before taking any plunges.'

'Where did you meet?'

'At the Victoria and Albert as a matter of fact.'

'I say, that's one of my favourite places.' Gushed Harriette.

'I rather like the Dickens' pen case.' Replied Ed.

'Oh, yes me too. I must say Dickens is one of my favourite authors. I think I have read every one of his novels.'

'We do have things in common. I am rather a Dickens tragic myself.'

'Do you enjoy reading?' She asked.

'Oh yes, I believe there is nothing better than snuggled up with a good tome beside a roaring fire preferably with a glass of red in hand.' Replied Harriette. She waved away a bee trying to land on her glass.

'I suppose you are quite tired of reading by the time you return home having all those manuscripts to plow through. I cannot imagine the stuff some people might write. There must be so much you relegate to the rubbish bin.'

Ed was currently working for a literary agent spending many hours perusing manuscripts sent in by aspiring authors in the hope that their work would be published. Her previous employment was with a publisher, a Mr Teesdale, but he did not think she was suitable for the task. It was not her forte he had told her, and had recommended she look for something else instead. It had been something of a blessing that she was finally let go as he had commenced making sexual advances towards her whenever she entered his office. His corpulence, yellow teeth and tobacco smell repulsed her, together with his walrus moustache in which seemed to lurk flecks of food. She thought he probably had dismissed her when she did not rise to his bait. To deter his lasciviousness, she had revised her wardrobe ensuring that her low cut blouses and tight skirts would only be worn after working hours and not in the office. She had been rather disillusioned about the publishing industry. She had surmised that editors and publishers spent time taking their authors to lunch in ritzy restaurants on the company expense account. She had broached the subject with Teesdale one morning when she was collecting the manuscripts.

'You have got quite the wrong idea.' He replied as he proceeded to shuffle papers on his desk. The desk was always messy. He said that it was organised chaos and he knew where everything was but Ed doubted that as he was always mislaying things, blaming everyone else in the office except himself when something could not be located, especially the pimply faced junior who was in charge of making the tea and scuttling around running errands. She suspected Teesdale of being an alcoholic having caught him more than once taking a swig from a brandy bottle which he secreted in his bottom drawer. He had even offered her some saying that 'It is for the nerves, you know, purely medicinal'. This she refused to believe as his ruddy complexion and alcohol laced breath first thing in the morning indicated otherwise. She had gleaned from the staff that he was divorced and Ed's imagination worked overtime imagining him living in a room in a dingy lodging house with only a cat for company.

'Too busy for all that palaver.' He continued. 'I usually bring my own lunch. Don't need anything fancy. One cannot beat a curried egg sandwich. Lunch is really only to stoke the boiler. Now, dinner is a different matter. I don't mind indulging in a good piece of steak and a glass of red.' Ed's eyes had been drawn to his moustache. He must have already eaten some of his sandwich as bits of egg were nestling in the bush. Just as well he did not lunch with authors as she was sure they would be quite put off their food.

'There are certainly some which do not make the cut.' Said Ed responding to Harriette's question. 'However, I do feel rather sorry for the authors. They spend so much of their time and energy on their work only to have it rejected.'

'I would not be sorry for them.' Harriette retorted, 'They should expect to be rejected. Not everyone can be Hemingway!'

Ed thought that comment was rather harsh. It was similar to what old Teesdale had told her. He said she was not ruthless enough and wasted too much time reading manuscripts right through to the end especially the ones which were mediocre. He had told her publishing was not a charity but a business and he frequently would not bother even reading the submissions as there were always too many to sort through. She had thought that was really beyond the pale. At least he could make sort of effort and at least read a few chapters of people's work.

'You were saying last night you worked in a bookshop.' Commented Ed.

'It helps with the finances.' Replied Harriette 'Mother is always on at me about my spending. She is from that generation who saved. But, I ask you, what is the use of that? I say live for the moment, one never knows what is around the corner especially after all that transpired in the last war.' She thought how her mother had railed when she had heard about the soirees she had hosted in her flat one, in particular, before which her mother had arrived for an unannounced visit and had found her daughter pushing pieces of duck liver through a sieve then liberally adding liberal quantities of brandy and dollops of butter to the mix.

'Harriette!' Her mother expostulated 'The extravagance!' I really don't know how you can afford such things. It is no wonder you are always running short of money. If your father knew how much you spent on entertaining, he would have a fit.'

She had ignored her mother's disdain and continued with the sieving and mixing. She could not care what her parents felt about her spending or anything else. This was her flat and she would serve and do what she liked. The pate receipt had been given to her when she had spent time in Paris. Her mother had thought that a bit of French culture would always put one in good stead for the future so she had placed her with an elderly aunt. She lived not far from the Pere Lachaise cemetery around which Harriette would wander inspecting the graves of the famous artists buried there, especially Oscar Wilde to whom she was endeared as she had been appalled at his treatment by the authorities. She had been enrolled in a French language course at the Sorbonne. However, her interest lay in the profligate smoking of Gauloises, imbibing red wine and indulging in illicit sex which was more freely available than in her own country. She loved the liberal attitude of the French towards sex. Nothing was too risqué and public displays of affection between the sexes was never frowned on but seemed to be encouraged. If such displays were manifested in Britain, one would be just about arrested for being an affront to public decency.

Paris was where she had her first lesbian encounter. Her aunt was acquainted with Gertrude Stein an American from Pennsylvania who belonged to the Parisian avant-garde and had introduced Harriette to her when they had happened upon each other in a cafe in Montmartre. Stein was an avid collector of art, fostering many up and coming artists and authors who flocked to her salon at 27 rue de Fleurus where she lived with her lover Alice B Toklas. Harriette had been quite intrigued by this larger than life figure who had made a name for herself on the Parisian scene and her unique way with words was to say the least somewhat intriguing. When Stein had invited her to one of the "at homes" which she held in the salon on Saturday evenings, Harriette felt herself immediately accepting. She had envisioned an apartment elegantly furnished with works of art carefully hung on the walls. However, when she arrived on that Saturday evening, she was sorely disappointed as the paintings seemed to be unfinished and were also hard to comprehend. She had never sighted such works. Her interest lay in the old masters, landscapes of country and still life, not these works which seemed to jar her senses. She lit a cigarette and helped herself to wine which was flowing freely among the assemblage.

A tall tow headed woman sidled up to her.

'Haven't seen you here before.' Said she. 'You a friend of the general's, (the moniker had been recently bestowed on Stein and the name had stuck) Toklas or neither of the two?'

'Stein, actually,' Harriette replied. 'My aunt is acquainted with her. We ran into her in Montmartre the other day and she told me to pop in.'

'Just like her. This place is an open house. She lets anybody in. One only has to knock at the door and is told to 'entrez -vous.'

'That is exactly what she said to me.' Laughed Harriette.

The woman extended her hand.

'Maddy, Maddy Orford.' She announced.

Harriette shook the proffered hand noticing her strong grip. It seemed to match her rather deep and throaty voice.

'Harriette Cavendish. Pleased to meet you.'

They found a sofa on which they managed to squeeze. There was now quite a crowd milling around discussing the merits of the paintings and she could hear the strains of a lively debate taking place near the fireplace. One of the disputants was the author Thornton Wilder, a regular attendee at Stein's salon.

Maddy turned towards Harriette. 'Cavendish, you say. You're not related to old Tony in the Ministry?'

Harriette met her gaze. 'Yes, as a matter of fact, he's my father.'

'Oh, and what do you think he would say if he knew his little girl was here amongst all this lot?'

'I really could not care.' Harriette replied trying to portray a semblance of sophistication by lighting another cigarette, crossing her legs and flicking back her hair.

'I belong to the Communist Party.' Announced Maddy suddenly as though to elicit shock and gauge her reaction.

Harriette had never met one of her ilk although she had heard her father mention a bit about them. How the Party had formed after the General Strike, the miners joining in their hundreds. The Labour Party had attempted to join but a couple of attempts had proved unsuccessful.

Harriette did not possess affiliations with any of the parties. Politics did not interest her. It was probably her way of rebelling against her parents, her father in particular with whom she had a bad relationship. He had molested her when she was a child only ceasing when she had reached puberty and she had a lock installed on her bedroom door. She had tried telling her mother the things he had been doing to her but she had dismissed it all as made up fanciful filth and refused to believe her.

'I'm afraid politics do not interest me,' replied Harriette 'I think I had enough of it when I lived at home.'

Maddy agreed with that remark and refilled their glasses.

She asked,

'And what are you doing over here, pray tell, away from hearth, home and Mother England?'

'Mother thought it would put me in good stead if I had a little French culture,' Harriette replied. 'She enrolled me in a language course at the Sorbonne.'

'And how is that going?' Maddy queried.

'Oh, so, so. It's rather boring actually.' she said stifling a pretend yawn. 'I much prefer to obtain culture in other ways if you know what I mean.'

The comment had piqued Maddy's interest. Throughout their conversation she had felt drawn to this enfant anglaise. She was something of an enigma. There was an innocence coupled with a maturity and a rebellious streak all intertwined.

They decided to partake of the food which was being handed around. Harriette tried some duck pate which she declared rather delicious determining to procure the receipt so she could attempt to one day make it herself.

She turned to Maddy.

'And what of you?' she asked. 'What is your story?'

Maddy returned her gaze noting the flecks of gold in her eyes and a green that was almost metallic. They seemed to beckon her. Yes, Maddy said, she had a story. The only daughter of a titled family, her father was the Marquess of Palham. Her mother, the Marchioness had died in an influenza epidemic ten years ago. Maddy had led a privileged life, being presented at Court, doing the season in London and riding to hounds on the family's estate in Northumberland. However, this way of life was not to her liking. She had found the people with whom she mixed all rather vacuous. They seemed to be concerned with only which parties they would attend and how much alcohol they could consume. The latter applied to the men some of whom in a state of inebriation would grope her at balls and parties then collapse into a comatose state until the dawn of morning. She had made up her mind to extricate herself completely from the scene. She had heard that some friends of her mother were travelling to Shanghai and she determined she would go with them. After some protestation her father gave her permission to go on the condition she would stay with her mother's friends and return to England in two months time. She had been overjoyed. She had read a lot about China especially Shanghai where life was lived on the edge. She would be able to live in a completely different culture and immerse herself in the exotic customs of the Chinese people. A thriving port city, Shanghai was known as the Paris of Asia and was a veritable supermarket of pleasure. Maddy had taken advantage of this and had indulged in all forms of sexual activities which were heightened by the smoking of opium which was freely available in the many dens she frequented. When her time was up in Shanghai she had returned to England with a determination to find herself digs as soon as possible and continue to live free from the constraints of her previous life with her father.

'Well, that is quite a story,' said Harriette after Maddy had completed her narration 'I'm afraid mine rather pales in comparison.'

Maddy leant towards Harriette and patting her knee replied, 'Your story is just beginning and I'm sure I could teach you a few things to liven it up.'

It was after a few more glasses of wine and conversation that Harriette left Stein's apartment with her newly found friend. They walked to Maddy's apartment where Harriette was introduced to some things about which she fantasised and others not even considered. Their friendship had lasted for a couple of months until Harriette decided she was bored with the relationship. She wanted to meet other people, people of her own age and she was tired of being dragged along to Party meetings at which Maddy hoped that her lover would be converted and become a comrade just like her. They had gone their separate ways with no animosity occurring and it was then that Harriette embarked on a series of relationships which had all ended in disaster.

'Oh, here comes Tom,' announced Ed.

'Hello there. Been relaxing?' He said on his approach.

'Yes, we have rather,' replied Ed.

'Harry and I have been enjoying a little chat,' she added. 'Did you enjoy your row?'

Tom settled himself on the rug next to Ed and helped himself to a bottle of ale and a chicken drumstick from one of the baskets.

'Yes, thanks,' he replied. 'It's been rather a while since I took an oar. Not since Cambridge I believe.'

'Oh, that long? Then it's a wonder you made it back to shore,' laughed Ed.

Following Tom's lead, the two women helped themselves to the chicken.

'What time are you considering heading back?' Ed asked Tom.

'I thought after lunch. There is a brief I want to go over tonight and I have to be in court early tomorrow.'

'Oh,' said Ed despondently inwardly thinking how much time he spent poring over documents and not enough time on her.

'Did you catch the train here Harry?' She asked.

'Yes, I did and I think I should be leaving the same time as you. According to the timetable, there should be one departing about 1.45.'

'Would you like to come with us? Offered Ed. 'We could take Harry, couldn't we Tom?'

'By all means,' he replied wiping his fingers on a linen napkin. 'There is room for one more in the old jalopy.'

'Oh, goodoh. If it won't be a bother.' Said Harriette.

'No bother at all. You would be most welcome.'

'So, that's settled,' said Ed.

'We will meet you out the front about 1.15.' Said Tom.

Before the maid commenced packing her suitcase, Harriette ensured that the stolen ring was still securely hidden in her toiletry bag. She had thought it was a good place in which to hide it nestled among her toothbrush, soap and flannel. Although the latter were usually provided for guests in the grand country houses, Harriette preferred to bring her own.

'Is that all madam?' Asked the maid as she folded the last item of clothing placing it in top of the others.

'What? Oh yes, that will do. Kindly have the case brought down,' said Harriette testily.

'Certainly madam.' Said the maid bobbing as she did so. Harriette glanced at her watch then looked through the window. The car was pulling up outside the front entrance.

She hurried down the staircase.

'Goodbye, and thank you. It was spiffing as always,' she gushed as Lady Salisbury proferred a rouged cheek which Harriette deftly managed to avoid.

'Quite alright my dear,' she trilled. 'You must come again. Maybe for the grouse.'

Harriette declined to reply.

Tom and Ed approached.

'Thank you so much Lady Salisbury for your hospitality,' said Ed. 'We had a marvellous time.'

'Yes, thank you,' echoed Tom. 'I'm sorry we have to leave so soon but I want to be in London no later than nine.'

'Oh, will it take that long?' Questioned Lady Salisbury. 'I cannot remember the last time I went to London.' She turned towards the butler.

'Benson, when was the last time I went to London?'

'London, my Lady? I cannot really recall. Maybe it was Ascot last year.'

'Last year?' She queried, her forehead puckering gravely 'No, I'm sure it was not last year. I was on the continent last year or, was that the year before?' 'Where has Albert got to, he might know when it was.' She cast her eyes around in a futile attempt to locate her aged husband but was informed by the butler that His Lordship had been last seen walking in the direction of the river with a fishing rod over his shoulder.

'Fishing? Why on earth has he gone fishing? He always wanders off when we have company. Did he say when he would be returning?'

'Sorry to interrupt,' announced Tom before the butler had an opportunity to reply, 'But we really must be going.'

Benson directed the footman to install the suitcases on the dickey seat as Tom, Ed and Harriette climbed aboard and the car moved off along the gravel drive, past the stands of massive oaks and on through the iron gates of the estate.

Harriette lit a cigarette and settled back in the seat.

'Thought we would never get away,' she commented. 'The old girl certainly likes to talk and her memory seems rather worse for wear. Methinks she is on the downhill slide.'

Ed turned her head and asked.

'Have you known her long?'

Harriette took a drag of her cigarette and looked through the window.

'Quite some time, father served with old Salisbury in the last war. He and mother used to trek up here quite often and then I started coming.'

'Do you hunt?' Asked Tom as he stopped the car allowing a tractor to pass. The farmer waved and they set off again.

'No, not I,' replied Harriette, 'I find it rather too boring, apart from the stirrup cup beforehand. All that dressing up and charging around in all weathers with barking dogs looking for foxes. No, I'm afraid I rather prefer to be in front of a fire with a good novel and a large glass of red.'

'So, you won't be coming up for the shoot?' Queried Ed.

'I have not given it much thought. Will you be going?'

'Will we go?' Asked Ed turning to Tom.

'It depends when it is. I have a few cases coming up and I might not be able to fit it in.'

'Oh. I was hoping we could go,' Ed said despondently. 'I heard it is quite fun and the ladies do not have to be involved with the shooting.'

Harriette interjected, 'You heard right. The ladies tend to ensconce themselves in the library being ministered to by the footmen bringing pots of tea and scones. 'Of course,' she added, 'there is always tennis and croquet if one is so inclined and there is a smashing fireworks display on the Saturday evening.'

'Oh, it all sounds super,' Ed gushed, 'I do love fireworks.'

Her interest was piqued. She would go even if Tom would not. She could easily catch the train up here and there would bound to be people with whom she could socialise. It was time she had a bit of fun without Tom. Lately all he seemed to think about were his damned court cases. Maybe she could coax her new friend Harry to go with her.

As they sped along through the glens, Harriette seemed to possess a telepathic sense of Ed's thoughts. She intuited that Ed was interested in going to the shoot. It would be an ideal opportunity for her to inveigle herself into Ed's favour without the encumbrance of that boring fellow Tom. She was unconcerned about the ring now, as it was obvious that old Salisbury would not remember if she had ever possessed it. Her eyes were drawn to the back of Ed's slender neck and she visualised what lay beneath that demure tweed skirt and twinset. She certainly had bigger breasts than Priscilla and her calves looked shapely enough. Oh yes, she was a ripe peach just ready for the picking and she would ensure that the room they shared contained a double bed for the seduction.

'I say' she announced, 'I rather think I will go up there. If you want to come Ed, and Tom can't go, then we can go there together.'

'Oh, really? That would be smashing. What do you think of that Tom?'

He changed into second gear as they ascended a hill.

'That's fine with me.' He answered.

'You can tell me all about it when you return.'

'Oh, I will,' Ed replied excitedly. 'Especially the fireworks display.'

Harriette thought, the only thing he will hear about will be the fireworks if everything goes according to my plan.

CHAPTER 9

1986

'Georgia,' called my aunt, 'Could you please plump my pillows? I cannot seem to get comfortable.'

She had slipped over in Waitrose breaking her hip and, because I was the youngest and only relation with whom she had somewhat of a rapport, (her son had been estranged from her many years ago and lived in Australia) she had summoned me back from Italy to care for her in her convalescence. I was sorry to leave however, my feelings were ambivalent. Returning to the UK would give me a needed bit of breathing space albeit having to look after my domineering aunt. The attack had left me feeling anxious and fearful as I had escaped with my life. Fortunately for me, before my fate was sealed, a couple of hikers had appeared on the trail and the attacker had fled. I did not report the incident to the police as I did not want anyone to know what had happened to me and I felt, however foolishly, that I did not want the incident to besmirch the beauty of the area. I thought about telling Maria but could not bring myself to do so. She had her own problems, and if she knew there was a rapist on the loose it might prevent her from venturing outside and leading a normal life.

'Georgia, are you coming?'

'Yes, auntie, I'm coming now,' I replied wishing that she would curb her demands as I walked up the stairs for the umpteenth time. I had entertained the idea of contacting a home care service and determined to broach the subject with her. However, I knew what the reaction would be. She would not want a stranger in her home 'poking around in my affairs and pilfering the silver.' It was not as though she could not afford to employ someone either as she was rather well off. My uncle had been a leading Harley Street cardiologist saving many hearts of the upper echelons of society. Ironically, he had died from cardiac arrest, his funeral attended by the grateful patients he had saved and who had paid the fees which funded his and his wife's lifestyle in this classy flat on the Marylebone Road.

'Now, Georgia,' she announced, 'I thought it might be a good idea to have a bell on the table beside me. Then I would not have to shout for you when I need something. What do you think?'

'Oh, a bell? I queried as I plumped up the pillows inwardly thinking that this was the last straw. She would be constantly summoning me like a servant forever at her beck and call.

I ventured, 'You know, I was thinking you might be better off with someone who is more suited to the task of caring for people. Someone better than I. Like a nurse for instance.'

'A nurse?'

'Yes. She would not need to live in, she could come for a few hours every day.'

'But you know I don't like strangers in the house Georgia. It is enough that Potts comes in to do the rough, and', she wheedled, 'You are doing such a good job looking after me.'

'Thank you, auntie, but you know I cannot stay here forever. I will have to return to Italy. I still have the lease of the cottage in Portovenere.'

'I really do not know why you had to go all the way over there just to dispose of Wina's ashes,' she said rather petulantly her hands smoothing the 1,000 thread Egyptian cotton sheet. 'You could have disposed of them here.'

My father's sister, my aunt Mavis, did not possess much empathy towards others and, in particular, my mother whom she thought had made life hard for my father with her moods and depression. On more than one occasion, she had even accused her of malingering and seeking attention.

I ignored her comment as I knew it would only end in a slanging match if I tried to justify myself. I cast about for another subject.

'Have you heard from the solicitor?' I asked.

She had instituted legal proceedings against Waitrose as she claimed that her fall had been due to spilt detergent which had not been removed from the floor.

'Yes,' she replied. 'As a matter of fact, he is supposed to be calling in this afternoon with the papers for me to sign.'

By now I had walked over to the window. The view was a Victorian church, great bare plane trees between the houses, three or four chimney pots and, through the mews, going about their daily lives a few people meandered. I wondered about my friends in Portovenere, what were they doing now, and my little cottage, now empty. I was impatient to return and recommence my research, not here being treated like a dogsbody by my aunt.

Her voice impinged on my thoughts.

'I need to look my best you know.'

'Georgia, are you listening to me?'

'What? Oh, what were you saying?'

'I said, I will want to look my best to receive Mr Cowdrey. Now, I was thinking about wearing my lemon lace bed jacket, you know the one I bought in Venice. I hope you have washed it separately with the Lux flakes as I instructed and that stain is removed. I don't know where it came from unless I spilt some soup the last time I wore it.'

I had washed the jacket this morning but had neglected to use the flakes. Instead, I had thrown it in the machine with the other washing and had then bundled the lot into the drier where it was now tumbling around on a high heat. I had to rescue it before it was ruined and I would have to incur her wrath.

'I just remembered, I think I left the iron on.' I blurted out as I dashed from the window past her bed and down the stairs to the laundry leaving any forthcoming castigation dangling on her tongue. Opening the door of the dryer, I extricated the jacket. It had tangled with a pair of aunt's commodious bloomers but, apart from being a little damp, it appeared to pass muster and the stain had thankfully disappeared. That was probably due to the normal detergent and not those flakes which I had been instructed to use, was my thought as I closed the dryer door to finish off drying the rest of the washing. I hung the jacket on a hanger placing it near the window where there was a shaft of sunlight and hoped the solicitor was arriving much later as it would give the jacket time to dry.

Her voice assailed my ears again. What does she want now for goodness sake? Probably wanting to know about the iron, how long and how many times it had been left on unattended. I made my way upstairs thinking how I had to get away from here. She was driving me to distraction.

'How long does it take you to turn off an iron?' She demanded as soon as I entered her room.

'I had to check on the washing in the drier.'

'I certainly hope you did not put anything delicate of mine in the drier. You should know that things tend to shrink in those things.'

'No, I didn't aunt,' I lied thinking about her lacy confection being thrown around with her bloomers and I felt the humour of it and had to suppress a giggle which threatened to undo me.

'Just as well then. 'And,' she continued warming to her theme. 'In future, please remember not to leave the iron on. It is very dangerous. At your age, Georgia, you should know better. If you had gone out when it was left on, the place could have caught fire and I would have been burnt to death in my bed.' She expostulated.

Before I had time to reply, she put in her order for lunch and demanded that the crusts be cut off the bread which was to be sliced squarely and not on the angle as I had cut the toast this morning. She requested lunch early so she could digest it properly before Mr Cowdrey put in his appearance which was going to be sooner than I had hoped. I thought about the jacket, how it would dry, then I thought about my hair dryer. I could use it to eliminate any last vestiges of dampness lurking in the garment.

As I put her soup on to boil and buttered the bread her words of chastisement rattled in my brain and fury clasped my throat. How dare she speak to me like that? Who does she think is? I was a grown woman, not a child and had been living independently for many years. I determined that after the solicitor had gone, I would ring the Agency and have a nurse or carer installed here as soon as practicable whether my aunt agreed to my proposal or not.

CHAPTER 10

1926

On the weekend of the grouse shoot in the confines of Henley Hall, Harriette had wasted no time in encouraging Ed to share her bed surrendering to Harriette's charms and sexual prowess. They had gone together as Harriette had planned as Tom had opted to say put amongst his clot of legal papers. However, Ed had experienced a feeling of guilt about deceiving Tom whom she did like, perhaps, even love. It was all so confusing she had felt herself saying to Harriette as she lay beside her after another orgasmic delight.

'Buck up and have some of this.' Harriette said offering her snuff box of cocaine.

'It's just the thing for making one forget about the quandaries of life.'

It was the first time she had offered the drug to Ed. Although she herself was a regular user she felt rather a protectiveness towards her protégé. She wanted her to maintain that childlike innocence which was what had attracted her in the first place. But at this moment, the drug might be what was needed to take Ed's mind off her relationship problem. Harriette did not want to lose her completely to Tom. She would try and convince her that it was possible to conduct two relationships at the same time. But Ed was young and finding her way and not as experienced as Harriette. It was not going to be easy but it would be worth Harriette's efforts of persuasion and it would be a challenge. She was always partial to a challenge.

'I feel rather louche,' announced Ed sprawled naked on the sheets. There was a flush to her cheeks, her dark hair pooling around her.

'Does this stuff make one feel like that?' She asked.

'Quite possibly.' Harriette replied thinking that was just how she wanted her to feel, louche and uninhibited, with no qualms about sleeping with her and that solicitor.

'You know,' murmured Ed stroking Harriette's arm. 'I could get used to this life.'

'What? The life as in living here at the Hall or as we are now, just the two of us here together.'

'Oh, I rather think the whole jolly lot.'

'Well, I don't envisage ever living in a place such as this, however the second option is a definite possibility.'

'I wonder what Tom would say if he knew I was in bed with you.'

'No more talk, time for sleep.' Harriette responded abruptly cutting her off before she could mention anything else about him. She reached over and turned off the lamp.

'Sleep tight,' she said.

'You too.'

However, it took Ed quite some time to do that. The cocaine she had inhaled earlier had left her feeling somewhat edgy and restless and she lay awake her mind a jumble of thoughts and emotions. What was she doing? Was she truly a lesbian? She did not imagine she was as she still had feelings for Tom, even thought she would one day marry him, but Harriette had unearthed something in her, something of which she was not aware until that first time she had slept with this person who was snoring beside her. She was so attracted to her and the sex was much better than what she had with Tom. He was one of those wham, bam, thank you mam types and did not know what really excited her. But maybe she was to blame for that. Maybe she should jolly well tell him what she liked but she felt rather shy about saying anything. She thought he might think ill of her and think she was some sort of scarlet woman, but what was she now, for goodness sake? Harry seemed to know everything there was to know about sex and did not need Ed to guide her. She could have Harry for her sexual needs and Tom could provide her with whatever Harry could not. The more she thought about Harry's suggestion of maintaining two relationships the more she thought it might work. Tom already was occupied with his legal practice, working long hours often through the night. And they were not living together yet however she thought that might change if they were to become engaged. He had intimated as much when they were ensconced in bed one night and he had settled back with a post coital cigarette.

'How would you feel about giving up your digs and moving in with me?'

'Living with you?' Ed had replied rather taken aback by the suggestion. She rather liked where she lived, her flat in St Johns Wood. Although it was small it was her place, a place where she had freedom to come and go as she liked. A place where she could entertain who she liked and get up when she liked, even to stay in her pyjamas all day and listen to her favourite programs on the wireless or her records on the gramophone, sometimes dancing uninhibited to a song which took her fancy. And what of her pet canary who tended to be noisy and was now commencing to talk? She knew it would drive Tom mad if he had to put up with that on a regular basis. The last time he had visited he commented how noisy it was and he found it hard to concentrate on the crossword. If she moved in with him, she would have to relinquish that and she did not feel she could do it right now. His apartment was at Holland Park. Although it was a larger apartment than Ed's, it tended to be rather dark resulting in lamps having to be turned on during daylight hours. Although he had a weekly who came to clean or, supposedly clean, as Ed had caught her on more than one occasion with her feet up on the table beside a cup of tea, cigarette in hand reading a woman's magazine. 'Just havin' a break lovey', her words of explanation, which of course Ed had not believed. She had told Tom about her tardiness but he still kept her on as she was an old friend of his mother's and was having a hard time. His tidiness was anathema to Ed who liked everything awry. All her books higgledy piggledy on the bookshelf as well as her clothes stuffed into the wardrobe, falling off the hangers and her underwear jammed into the drawers. His clothes were sorted into seasons and occasions, suits and jackets in one section, shirts and ties in another. No, she could not envisage it. She would have to stall him.

'Oh, I think we are good the way we are' she replied brightly. 'You know what they say, familiarity breeds contempt and absence makes the heart grow fonder.'

'I thought you would like to live with me,' he said rather dejectedly. 'Isn't that what people do who love each other. They want to be together' 'And,' he added to give more weight to his argument, 'It is rather quite de rigeur now as you well know.'

'Yes, Tom, I acknowledge all that but, for the moment, I want things to go along as they are. Can't we just enjoy each other's company before we make any serious commitment? I want to experience life a bit more before I marry you or anyone else.'

'Anyone else?' He exclaimed rather testily. 'Have you got someone else waiting in the wings?'

'No, of course not silly,' she had said ruffling his hair.

'Now, how about we talk about this some other time? I can feel the beginnings of a headache.'

And that was where they had left it, the subject of commitment. She had wished he had never mentioned it but knew it was bound to rear its ugly head sooner or later.

Now here she was on holidays winging her way with Harry to some obscure place in Italy, Tom electing not to come his usual workload preventing it. However, he was hopeful of joining them at the end of their stay which caused Ed quite some perturbation. How long would he stay? How would that work the three of them together? Would there be a menage a trois? She could never imagine that eventuating. His suspicions were sure to be aroused.

Ed had not heard of this Italian place until Harry had gushed about it one day over tea and scones in the cafe of the London Library.

'Oh, Eddy, you'll love it. I've been there. It's a tiny village called Portovenere on the Ligurian sea. Everyone who's anyone has been there.'

'Who, for instance?' Queried Ed dolloping a good portion of cream onto her scone.

'Well,' she replied enthusiastically. 'Virginia Woolf, Hemingway, Byron and Shelley. Byron even has a grotto named after him. Apparently, he completed quite a marathon swim around those parts. And,' she added. 'We have the use of a cottage which is owned by a friend of my father.'

Ed listened with interest. She and Harry were both quite fond of Byron, in particular, 'She Walks in Beauty,' a poem which she thought encapsulated everything about love and romance. Harry had quoted a few lines to her one day as they walked beside a bickering river in Oxford: "Meet in her aspect and her eyes, thus mellowed to that tender light, which heaven to gaudy day denies".

Tom was not as romantic and his love for poetry was not as keen as hers however, he was caring and non-judgmental and they both shared the same sense of humour. She was torn between the two, Harry and Tom, Tom and Harry. A holiday in Italy was appealing. They would be staying in a stone cottage at the top of a cliff under which was the grotto of Byron.

She said. 'But I would have to ask old Teesdale if I could take leave.'

'Of course,' replied Harry. 'But I hardly think it would be a problem. You said you are owed holidays and I thought you said there was another employee starting next week.'

'Yes, that's right, although you know what he can be like. I shall have to get him at the right moment.'

'Just wear one of your low-cut blouses and lean over his desk a few times. That should put him in the right mood,' she smirked 'and, as for me, I dare say the shop will manage quite well without me. I am only there part time as it is.'

The library was one of their favourite meeting places both feeling it would not raise anyone's suspicions. After all, it was the place Ed often frequented employed as she was in the publishing industry so, even if by chance Tom had gone there and seen her with Harry, he would not have thought anything untoward about it. What could be more normal than two women friends meeting there among the books which they both loved? In the confines of the establishment there were many nooks which they had sought, nooks in which their feelings for each other were demonstrated albeit surreptitiously. Initially, it was the gazing of eyes, Harry's constantly bewitching Ed with their metallic flecks. There were whispers of love, brushing of lips and furtive fumblings under desks or behind bookcases. Then, after a time, their assignations became bolder and more daring even once coming close to being discovered by one of the staff as Harry's tongue was slipping into her lover's mouth.

They had gone away for a couple of weekends to Sussex staying in a cottage owned by Bunny Garrett who was a former member of the Bloomsbury group and also a friend of Harry's. Harry had said that he had had a falling out with John Nash who had accused him of pilfering a piece of pottery when he had stayed at Charleston. He had vehemently denied the charge but felt that the thrown mud had stuck and, in his words, 'they all could get fucked'. Tom had not put up any protestation when Ed had told him she was going to Sussex as he was once again immersed in a protracted case. He thought it would do Ed good to get out of the London smog and imbibe some country air with her friend. Knowing Tom would be unable to come she had extended an invitation for him to join them although feeling rather guilty as she had said it but at the same time relieved when he had declined. However, her relief was short lived as he had said he might be able to get away for a few hours on the Sunday depending on how soon he was able to complete his work.

Nestled in among an overgrown garden the small brick and flint cottage was outside the village of Glynde. Ed had been entranced when they had arrived after Harry had driven them down from London in her Vauxhall.

'Oh Harry, there is even a pond!' She had exclaimed, making her way through the undergrowth, 'And apple trees!'

Harry having stayed here before, did not share her lover's enthusiasm and commenced unloading the luggage from the car.

She called out.

'Hey, come here and help me with these cases. There's plenty of time to explore.'

Ed returned picking off some prickly thorns which had managed to cling to her skirt. She picked up her case and followed Harry who was bending down and extracting a key from underneath a cracked terracotta pot which now only contained some wizened stalks of flowers which had long ago ceased to bloom.

'Looks as though there has not been anyone here for ages.' Commented Ed after they had entered and she had noticed the ceiling draped with cobwebs and a layer of dust on the old kitchen table.

'Yes, it does, my pet, quite a while I would say,' replied Harry. She had started calling her that lately and Ed found she rather liked it: Harry's pet. Even Tom did not call her that. The closest he would come would be dear or dearest, both words making her feel like some sort of geriatric and she was a long way off that. No, she thought pet suited her rather nicely.

'We will have to get cracking and clean the place before we unpack,' Harry continued, making her way to the cupboard under the sink hauling out scrubbing brushes, carbolic soap and some old wash cloths which had seen better days.

'Have a look out the back,' she threw over her shoulder. 'There should be a bucket near the door.'

Ed went out and found the bucket containing dirt and something indeterminate. She sluiced it under a nearby tap. The water which gushed had a rusty brown colour and she imagined taking a bath in it. She had not envisaged having to clean the cottage and felt rather resentful at having to do so. She had thought it would be spic and span, all ready for their enouncement. She thought it was rather rude of that fellow who owned the place. The least he could have done was to tidy it up for guests but then Harry had said he told her she had to take it as she found it and, after all, he was not charging them anything to stay there for the weekend. She had supposed that was a bonus.

As they commenced sweeping, scrubbing and dusting, Ed found her previous resentful feelings slowly vanishing. Here she was with Harry, her lover being domestic, keeping house. She looked over at her now on her hands and knees scrubbing the floor her cheeks flushed with exertion and mottled with dirt not caring what she looked like. In that moment Ed felt an overwhelming surge of love so powerful she would have been at a loss to explain it to anyone let alone to Harry.

The weekend had passed in a blur of activity. On the Saturday, they had walked along the ridge of the downs to witness the rising of the sun, their shoes wetted with the dew christened grass. They had been pummelled by a wind so fierce Ed had feared they would be blown right off the cliff. A nearby deserted beach had seen them braving the water's chill as, like two naughty children on a seaside holiday, they had frolicked and splashed until the sun had lost its warmth. Harry had brought with her a tablecloth with which she covered the scrubbed pine table. Ed had filled an old jam jar with a bunch of wildflowers she had picked from the garden and there they had sat partaking of simple meals concocted mainly by Harry whose culinary skills surpassed those of her lover. They had picked the ripe apples off the trees and sat on the grass unperturbed about the juice trickling down their chins.

It was in the small hours of Sunday morning, the time before the birds commenced their chorus, that Ed lay awake as Harry slept soundly beside her. It was amazing to her how Harry slept. It seemed as soon as her head hit the pillow she would be snoring whereas she would lie awake ruminating about all the things which had occurred during the day and things which would or might occur in the future. At this moment her mind was a jumble of thoughts about the life she was living and how she could maintain it. Today Tom was coming. He had rung the post office and left a message which was dispatched by the postmistress' sullen son who had expected a monetary reward for his efforts. The message had stated that he was due to arrive around lunchtime and Ed had suggested they get away from the cottage which she felt held too much of their cohabitation. She thought Tom would be able to smell the aromas of their amative activities and also the drug they had been inhaling. She would have to tell Harry she did not want to take that any longer. Although she enjoyed the way it heightened her senses and made sex more enjoyable she disliked the after effects. It always made her feel edgy and restless and blew her problems out of all proportion.

They had elected to have a picnic, the provisions having been purchased from one of the shops in the village after their skinny dip on Saturday. They would carry the basket of goodies into one of the nearby meadows where a couple of hours could be whiled away on a rug under the shade of one of the many beech trees which were dotted around the countryside. Afterwards, a walk could be taken and the guest shown the view towards Newhaven from one of the ridges the lovers had traversed.

Upon arrival at the cottage, Ed had greeted Tom with as much affection she thought was permissible knowing Harry was right behind her. Afterwards on the rug she found she was uncertain where to put herself. Should she sit close to Harry or Tom? Either way, one of them would feel rejected so she decided to sit in the middle, turning her head this way and that meeting their gaze. She hoped that they both would feel they were receiving her full attention, hanging on their every word, laughing at appropriate times and commiserating at others. Thankfully, the conversation was mainly about Tom's forthcoming court case, he very confident his client would be found not guilty of the charge brought against him. 'It is a prima facie case of self defence.' Tom had said responding to Harry's question. 'And,' he added, 'I've briefed one of the best QC's in the business.' He had naturally questioned them about their activities, what they had been doing, where they had gone and so on. Ed had felt rather uncomfortable having to answer his questions the images of her and Harry's bedroom romps always at the forefront of her mind. Ed had ensured the door of the room was closed prior to his arrival as she was certain his suspicions would have been aroused if he had observed the double bed and not two singles. Harry had told her not to be so uptight and sensitive about the situation. She intimated that he could jolly well like it or lump it. But Ed was not to be swayed. She had deftly manoeuvred him from the front door straight into the small living room, plying him with tea and biscuits before they set off for their picnic.

'I say, what about a photo?' Harry exclaimed after they had had their fill. She produced the box brownie camera which accompanied her nearly everywhere she went. Her interest in photography was keen and she had taken a few of Ed which Ed had thought could be classified as soft porn. However, Harry had told her it was 'just art darling' and 'I want to remember you just like this' as she had positioned her on the bed with a sheet barely covering her nether regions and her breasts displayed to full advantage. She seemed to have some sort of hold on her and Ed seemed powerless to stop it.

Tom suggested he would take a photo of the two women but Harry said he should be in the photo also. Ed suggested she would take one of Tom and Harry and Harry could then take one of Ed and

Tom. Back and forth they went, 'You be in it, no you'. The dilemma had been averted by the assistance of a passing farmer who had been only too happy to take a photo of the group. 'Nice day for a picnic, I reckon. A special occasion is it?' He asked his eyes roaming over the remnants of the repast in particular the empty bottles of hock dejectedly lying beside the basket. 'Oh no, we were just enjoying some of this lovely country air.' Ed quickly said wishing that he would take the photo and be on his way and not engage them in more conversation leading to more questions which she wished to avoid. All she wanted was for Tom to depart back to London and preferably on his own. He had intimated during the course of the visit he would like Ed to accompany him. She had as yet to let him know. She had after all come with Harry and presumed and thought it would be right that they would drive back together. She had acquiesced finally and gone back with him pointing out to Harry while he waited in the car that after all they would soon be spending time together in Italy. But Harry was not easily mollified and had waved them off the feelings of resentment and anger barely contained. It had taken a telephone call and a dinner at a rather classy restaurant which Ed had shouted to bring her back into Harry's favour.

11
CHAPTER

'Good afternoon ladies and gentlemen,' trumpeted the air hostess. 'We will soon be arriving at Leonardo da Vinci airport. Please return to your seats and fasten your seatbelts, thank you.' The Imperial Airways plane was en route from London to Rome. Among the thirty two passengers on board were Harriette and Ed, the latter suffering the effects of airsickness, vomiting into the bowl supplied whenever the turbulence became severe. Although the passengers were well rugged up, it was still cold on board and was also very noisy as the crew used the megaphones to relay any pertinent messages.

Harriette had encouraged Ed to travel with her to Italy. She realised she was the one she wanted to be with, her capriciousness seeming now to have disappeared. She felt an affection for her, an affection she did not have with her other lovers. Was it love? She was not sure but Ed was the one she wanted to share these weeks abroad in Italy, in Portovenere, her favourite place, the place where the artists stayed, wrote and painted, where in that inky sea Byron had swum. Yes, they would go together, removing themselves from the fug of London and the gossiping hordes and instead savour the sights, sounds and food for which Italy was famous. The Italian cuisine was what she adored, the pastas, the veal, the prosecco and chianti preferably consumed alfresco under a setting sun.

'Well, I will certainly be glad to be on terra firma.' Commented Ed as she turned towards Harry who was placing her book in her bag and buckling the seat belt.

'Yes, you poor pet, I must say I have never seen anyone be so ill on a plane,' she replied patting her hand.

'I don't know why I was so sick,' said Ed who also fastened her belt. 'Usually,' she explained, 'I only feel nauseous, not vomiting like that. It must have been that sandwich I had at the airport. Come to think of it, it didn't taste very fresh'.

'God,' she added, I must look a fright.'

She withdrew from her bag a compact the mirror of which confirmed her fears. There were hemispheres under her eyes and her creamy complexion was reduced to a sickly pallor. To try and improve matters she rolled on some lipstick as the plane commenced its descent through the clouds. She prayed she would not again require the sick bowl. Landing was something she always dreaded, visualising the plane crashing to the ground, the injured or dead passengers strewn around as in a war zone.

There was another passenger sitting at the rear of the plane who also had the same fear. It was Ernest who had been assigned to cover Il Palio di Sienna, the horse race festival held annually at Piazza del Campo in Sienna He had elected to go in place of Jim who had been admitted to hospital with appendicitis. Ernest had looked forward to this trip abroad. Even though he would be working he had taken his holidays to afford him more time to enjoy himself. He looked forward to getting away for a while from the drear of London with its days pregnant with smog and lacking the warmth of the sun. In Italy the sun would be intense. He thought there was nothing like it to lift one's mood. It would be just the tonic he needed. Since his breakup with Harriette he had not bothered with a serious relationship. His love life mainly consisted of one- night stands and a couple of blind dates which one of his journalist friends had arranged. Both dates had been failures. The first one had nothing to talk about apart from constantly disparaging her ex boyfriend and the other had been so monosyllabic Ernest had to plead a migraine and miss out on the trifle which he had spotted on the menu and was his favourite dessert. He had hopes of maybe meeting someone in Italy. He knew the Italian women were quite sexy and family orientated. He just hoped he could communicate with them as his Italian only consisted of the basic words like "bongiorno, ciao and amore." However, he had borrowed a phrase book from Jim so he could refer to that whenever he needed which he mused, was going to be rather a lot.

To Ed's relief, the plane landed safely and, after clearing customs, the women retrieved their bags. With Harry's arm under Ed's, she trotted her out into the heat and tumult of Rome and into a waiting taxi both of them unaware that Harry's ex- boyfriend had been on the same flight. He had headed to the nearest public lavatory where he stayed until his stomach settled and all traces of nausea had vanished.

CHAPTER 12

1986

My aunt had contracted a flu virus which she said I must have brought to the house. 'Probably from that Italian place where you stayed,' she had wheezed. 'Those foreign parts have the most dreadful germs,' she added giving weight to her misplaced theory. She had overlooked the fact that Potts, her cleaner had arrived one day with a runny nose however I could not be bothered alerting her to the fact.

I had contacted an agency and secured the services of a nurse, a Filipino, as I was finding aunt's care was becoming too much for me. Initially she had railed against the idea but, as the weeks passed, a weird friendship had developed between the two of them and I had felt a feeling of exclusion as time continued on. It did not worry me unduly as at least I had more time to myself and was not suffering her irascibility. However, I felt there was something not quite right about the situation, the way this woman was always going above and beyond the call of duty. Her behaviour was sycophantic, fawning over my aunt as though she was a blood relative and keeping me at arm's length. I intuited there was something conspiratorial occurring between them and then to justify my concerns, I found out that the solicitor was due to arrive tomorrow as per aunt's instructions in order to change her will. I voiced my concerns to an old friend of mine with whom I had arranged to meet at a coffee bar in Devonshire Street.

'In one way,' commented Margo 'I suppose you should be grateful she is taking over the reins. 'She certainly sounds such a harridan the way she treats you.'

'Yes, I know,' I replied toying with the spoon the barista had placed beside my cappuccino. 'but she's my only surviving relative and that woman is taking advantage of her. I'm sure she had something to do with the idea of changing her will.'

'Was she leaving anything to you?' she asked.

'Oh, I don't know. She has never spoken about it and I have never asked.'

Margo said. 'I remember you telling me that she is estranged from her son so I can't imagine she would be leaving him anything. I suppose if she has left this nurse her money you could contest the will. I mean, she hardly knows the woman. It's just too ridiculous.'

I sipped my coffee and thought that of course it was ridiculous. When the solicitor arrives tomorrow I will voice my concern about the situation. Surely, he would agree that it was not right.

Margo broke through my thoughts. 'Anyway, enough of your aunt. Tell me all about Italy. Have you managed to unearth anything about your mother and are you going back?'

While staying in London I had rung Margo. We had been friends at school but only caught up occasionally. I was indebted to her parents who used to take me with them when they holidayed on a dairy farm outside Chester. They were aware of my unhappy home life and thought it would do me good to get away from the situation even if it was for only a couple of weeks. I so looked forward to these holidays, writing and rewriting lists of the clothes I would take and visualising in bed at night all the fun I would have for the two weeks on the farm.

I scooped some foam off my coffee and told her about the little cottage in Portovenere, my eagerness to return and resume my quest. I told her about the photos I had unearthed, in particular, the one of mother and the woman with PV scribbled on the back. I told her about my Italian friends but did not tell her anything about the assault. I knew what her reaction would be. She would berate me and call me silly for not going to the police and making a report. We ordered Danish pastries and stayed for about an hour in which she apprised me of her life. Happily married for seven years to Peter a sales manager for Orchard fruit juices. They had a little boy called Hamish who had just commenced school and he was going to have a little sister or brother in six months time. She proudly produced a photo of them. I felt a frisson of sadness and wished I could have what my friend had, a family and someone with whom to share things? Was this to be my life? Working in a library, living with a cantankerous old aunt, my only interest trying to unearth my mother's past, a past which probably would not be as interesting as I thought it would be.

'A penny for them,' Margo said putting away the photo in her bag.

'What?'

'You looked like you were miles away and had lost your last penny.'

'Oh, don't mind me, I was just thinking how lucky you are.'

'Me? Lucky?'

'Yes, you seem to have everything, a loving husband, a beautiful son and another baby on the way.'

'Oh, well, thanks, but don't think it is all a bed of roses. We have our ups and downs just like everyone else. Bills to pay, the mortgage, work, morning sickness and Hamish has just been diagnosed with ADHD, not to mention an infection of nits!'

I did not anticipate that response so all I could offer was a grimace.

'Will he have to take medication?' I queried

'What, for the nits?'

'No, for the ADHD,'

'Oh, that, yes, it looks like it. I took him to our GP and he recommended that we put him on Ritalin although I am totally against it. I'm sure it is just a phase he is going through and will hopefully grow out of.'

'Have you had a second opinion?'

'We have an appointment next week with a child psychologist.'

'Oh, well good luck. I hope there is a better alternative and as you say it may just be a phase after all.'

Margo consulted her watch.

'Sorry, Georgie, I really must fly. If I'm not there on the dot of three Hamie will be in tears'. I will ring you.'

Outside the weather had changed. There was a gusty wind and a gloom had gathered about the trees. In misty rain, we farewelled each other promising to catch up when I returned from Italy. As I watched her drive away to collect her son, I opened my umbrella and set off for home wondering what would confront me when I arrived.

CHAPTER 13

My aunt had died in the early hours of a morning after my meeting with Margo, and the morning when the solicitor, Mr Cowdrey, had been due to come to change the will. I had woken to sounds of shouting coming from aunt's room and hastened to investigate. I found the Filipino cursing and punching my aunt who was lying comatose on the bed.

'What's going on?' I shouted horrified, 'What do you think you're doing?' I grabbed her and pushed her away and she fell to the floor.

There was no sign of life and I knew aunt was dead. My God, I thought surely she had not killed her?

'Stay where you are and don't move.' I yelled as the Filipino cowered in the corner. Frantic, I raced over and locked the door. Shocked, my fingers fumbled with the mobile but I managed to contact the police and also aunt's doctor who said would come over immediately. The nurse was now crying and I was unable to tell if they were tears of fear of being arrested or tears of disappointment of missing out on the windfall which she thought had been due to her. I wanted to close aunt's eyes which were still scarily open but I thought if it was a crime scene it would be better if I did not touch the body. I also wanted to pull up the sheet to cover her but that could not be done either. I would just have to wait until help arrived.

The minutes ticked by. I had one eye on the Filipino and the other focused on the window as I tried to see if someone was coming. Oh, please make them hurry, I prayed. I could not stand it much longer. It was bad enough to be in a locked room with a dead body let alone with a murderer if that is what this nurse was. I hoped and prayed it would not be the case but I looked around the room to see what I could use as a weapon if she decided to attack me. The visions of my attack in Cinque Terre flashed through my mind. Surely the odds of being set upon a second time were low. I noticed the vase on the bedside table and also the lamp but I hoped I would not have to use them as I did not relish the thought of bashing her over the head.

Through the window I spotted a police car pulling up outside. As per instructions, I ensured the nurse was locked in the room while I went downstairs to let them in.

'She's locked in the room with my aunt.' I told them as they followed me up the stairs.

When they entered the room they confronted the splotchy faced culprit who was now standing wringing her hands. She looked rather forlorn and in halting English gave an account of what had transpired. No, I heard her say, lady was dead, I did not kill. I try to rouse her, wake her up. She certainly had a brutal way of rousing a patient, I thought to myself as visions of her punching my aunt surfaced in my mind. There sounded a ring at the door and I excused myself to the detectives telling them it was probably the doctor. When I opened the door, it was not only the doctor but Mr Cowdrey was also on the doorstep.

I ushered them up the stairs and into the room where they were apprised by the police of the situation. The body was to be conveyed to the mortuary where an autopsy would be performed to confirm the cause of death. The Filipino was apparently free to go however, she would have to be available for any further questioning and could not leave the country until the matter was resolved. I apologised to the solicitor for not ringing him to cancel his appointment however he understood the circumstances and was also quite shocked at what had transpired. After the body had been transported from the house, the detectives had completed their enquiries and the doctor had departed (his professional opinion was heart failure probably due to pneumonia), I broached the subject of the will with the solicitor. He did not seem to think it was an unusual situation that aunt would be changing her will nearly on her death bed. He told me it was all perfectly legal for a person to change a will if that was what that person wished. However, he advised that if it could be proven in court there had been undue influence occurring then the will could be contested. He also told me that he was unaware of any evidence that his client was leaving anything to this nurse anyway so my worries were groundless and that due to aunt's death, the liability case against the supermarket would not now go ahead. He asked me if I knew my cousin's address in Australia so he could notify him and then gave me his business card. I was advised he would inform me regarding the result of the autopsy and the probate of the will.

They all departed including the nurse mumbling incoherencies as she packed her belongings and then disappeared out the door into the confines of a waiting taxi. My aunt, like a murder victim, enshrouded in a body bag, had been transported on a stretcher to the morgue. I was still in shock and my suspicions about the nurse had not been allayed. I had declined to take the doctor's offer of a sedative to tide me over. My cure lay in one of the bottles assembled on the butler's tray in the drawing room. I selected a Cognac and filled one of the brandy balloons. I sat back on one of the cream sofas and soon felt the warmth of the liquor soothe my shattered psyche. Up until now I had not had the time to really appreciate and savour this room as I was always too busy looking after aunt. I could not bear to think about what had transpired, she dead or maybe murdered, instead I tried focusing on my surroundings, on the silk lampshades, the rosewood table on which I had placed my drink, on the objects d'art carefully arranged around the room. It was certainly a very classy home. My mind segued into all the things which would be required to be done. The doctor had said that the autopsy should take only a few hours if there were no complications and then the funeral could be arranged. I hoped that it would be a simple procedure. I could not bear to think that she had been murdered by that nurse. It would be me who would have to organise everything; contact a funeral parlour and attempt to locate aunt's friends to advise them of her passing. Her clothes would need to be donated to charity or one of the second- hand clothing stores which dealt with designer labels of which aunt had been fond. I thought about the sorting of mother's clothes and wondered if aunt's would be imbued with that peculiar smell of old age.

Soothed by the brandy, I soon fell asleep. I dreamt I was in the sea in Portovenere. I was trying to save my mother and aunt from drowning but they were always just out of reach and being carried further out to sea. I tried screaming but no sound would come and then I heard ringing. Was it the bell of San Pietro tolling for the dead? In a sweat I awoke befuddled. Where was I? In Portovenere? No, I was here in Marylebone Road and the ringing was my mobile, in aunt's flat, my poor dead old aunt. Half drunk and half asleep I staggered over to the table where sat my phone.

'Hel, hello.' I slurred,

'Georgie, is that you?'

'Yes.'

'You sound different. It's Margo. Just wanted to know how things are?'

I sat down on the French reproduction chair trying to gather my wits. I was suddenly feeling the effects of the brandy. A migraine was threatening.

'Aunt's dead,' I blurted out.

'What, dead?' How, when?'

'Today, early.'

Then the enormity of what had happened descended on me and the tears which had remained until now unshed flowed unimpeded down my cheeks and onto my jeans.

'Georgie, are you alright?'

'N, not really.' I blubbed.

'Look.' Said Margo 'I am coming over there now. What is the address?'

Through my sobs, I managed to tell her the location then sat on the chair for awhile to compose myself. I made my way unsteadily to the guest bathroom where I splashed water on my face and searched around in the cabinet for some painkillers but all I found were some aspirin well past their use by date. I swallowed them anyway as I could not abide walking upstairs where aunt had died, and to my bedroom where my migraine tablets were kept. The mirror confirmed that I looked as bad as I was feeling. My hair was askew, my face was red and there were dark circles under my swollen eyes. I was past caring how I would look to Margo who was always so well groomed and who never went anywhere without makeup expertly applied, even now with a husband and a child to look after and pregnant into the bargain. I was running my fingers through my hair in an attempt to tame it when I heard the door.

'Georgie, I came as fast as I could.' Margo said after I ushered her in. 'You look terrible, you poor thing.'

Silently, I led the way into the drawing room and she sat down beside me on the sofa. She noticed the half empty bottle of brandy and the glass.

'Have you had anything to eat?' she asked cognisant of the fact that I had probably been drinking on an empty stomach.

'No, I haven't.' I whispered hardly able to meet her gaze 'Thanks for coming.'

'That's what friends are for.' She replied patting my hand. She stood up.

'How about I make us a sandwich or something? Just guide me to the kitchen. Then you can tell me all about what happened.'

I took her to the kitchen so glad to have someone in control. Rifling through the fridge, she came across some leftover ham and some butter and withdrew a half a loaf of bread from the bread crock while I procured a jar of English mustard from the pantry. Thank goodness there was some food in the house. I had planned to go to the supermarket today to replenish supplies but, because of the circumstances, there was no way that I would be foraying there. It would all have to wait until tomorrow. Margo set to work and soon the sandwiches were made and the cafetiere filled with coffee.

'I think we will eat it in here rather than that formal room.' She announced. 'It will be much cosier. What do you think?'

I agreed with her. In my present unkempt state, I would feel more comfortable talking to her here amidst the pots and pans and the accoutrements of a scullery.

I took two mugs from the cupboard, we settled ourselves at the pine table, and then summoning what energy remained I recounted all that had transpired: the discovery of the Filipino attacking the body of my aunt, the detectives arriving along with Mr Cowdrey and the doctor.

'My god, Georgie, it must have been horrific', Margo exclaimed as she poured the coffee. 'Do you really think that this nurse might have killed your aunt?' I mean it's just like something you might read in a crime book, an Agatha Christie novel.'

'I don't know what to think, Margo,' I replied drawing the mug towards me. 'I just hope she died from pneumonia as the doctor diagnosed.'

Margo took a bite of her sandwich.

'You said that the autopsy should not take very long. If everything's in order have you thought about the funeral? Will she be buried or cremated?'

Aunt had spoken to me about her funeral arrangements. She was to be cremated and her ashes placed with her husband in the same plot at East Finchley Crematorium. There was to be no religious service however she said she was rather partial to anything composed by Rodgers & Hammerstein. The only song I could think of which seemed remotely appropriate was "Alone Again". I mentioned this to Margo.

'What about, "There is Nothing Like a Dame"? from what I have heard about her that might hit the spot!'

We both started laughing and I found it was just what I needed, a good dose of mirth to quell the disquieting situation. I was sure aunt would approve of this choice of song.

'Would you like to come and stay with us tonight?' asked Margo after we had returned to normalcy.

'Oh, no, I couldn't impose on you like that.'

'It would be no trouble I assure you. There is a blow- up bed in the garage which Pete can inflate that is, if you don't mind sleeping on it.'

'No, thanks all the same Margo, but I think I will go back to my place.'

'Oh, ok, whatever you think is best, but if you change your mind just let me know.'

'Yes, I will. Thanks so much and thanks for coming over. You have been a brick.'

I stood up and collected the plates and mugs and took them over to the sink.

I looked at my watch.

'I had better not keep you any longer. It's nearly pick up time for Hamish.'

'Yes, it is.' Margo replied getting off the chair.

'I will just use the lavatory before I go.'

I directed her to the room in which I had splashed my face and then waited for her in the drawing room where she had left her bag. As I waited, I thought about going back to my flat. I had not been there since I departed for Italy. It was the only thing to do. I could not stay here tonight and sleep next door to where aunt had died and I did not want to impose on Margo. It was what I disliked at the best of times; imposing myself on people. I preferred to be independent as much as possible.

'All right?' I asked as Margo came into the room.

'Yes thanks. That should see me through until I get home. Ah, the joys of pregnancy,' she added retrieving her bag from the sofa, 'I seem to spend more time in the lavatory than anywhere else.'

I walked her to the door where we hugged with a promise that I would let her know the result of the autopsy and when the funeral would take place.

Ascending tediously up the stairs, it crossed my mind that I seemed to have had more than my share of deaths and funerals. First it was dad, then mother, a friend from work who died too young and now aunt. In the penumbra of my room as I packed my things into the suitcase my thoughts turned to the light and the warmth of Italy. Oh, how I missed it. In England, the days were growing shorter and it would soon be dark by 3.00pm. Today had been grey and windless with little distinction between clouds and sun. Last Spring was a mockery with the summer just as bad. I yearned to return to the little cottage in Portovenere which had been my home albeit for that small while. I had felt so connected to it as though it was where I had spent a previous life. But maybe it was the spirit of mother which was drawing me there, something akin to an umbilical cord, that connection to mother and child.

I descended the stairs with my suitcase and handbag, the migraine which I had managed to stave off commenced hammering at my skull. Entering the drawing room, my eyes alighted on the half bottle of brandy and the glass which I had neglected to put away. I placed the bottle on the butler's tray and took the glass into the kitchen and filling it with water, swallowed my migraine tablets which I had unearthed from my handbag. Rinsing the glass, I left it along with the crockery Margo and I had used. I knew Mrs Potts was due to come tomorrow so I scribbled a note about aunt's death and also my phone number should she want to contact me. She obviously would be shocked and out of a job but I was confident she would not have any trouble securing another one and I would provide a reference for her if she requested it. Then I phoned a taxi to transport me back to my flat in Fulham where I would stay until the funeral was held and my flight back to Italy undertaken.

CHAPTER 14

1927

They had stayed in Rome in a hotel in the district which was appropriately named, "The English Ghetto". It was where the aristocrats such as Wagner, Thackeray and Byron stayed while on their grand European tour and it had suited Harry and Ed perfectly. After unpacking, they had wandered around at their own pace imbibing of the brilliance of Rome. At the Piazza del Popolo, Harry had told Ed about the arch which had been carved by Bernini in honour of Queen Christina of Sweden. She had been a hunter, a scholar, wore pants, went on archaeological digs and was rumoured to have been a lesbian. This had Ed thinking again about her sexual orientation. Was she a true lesbian or just hedging her bets? She thought of Tom who was due to meet them in that place Harry enthused about. The place on the Ligurian sea, Portovenere. She hoped she would feel better by then as she was still experiencing bouts of nausea about which she had tried to keep from her lover, putting it down to the foreign food they were consuming. She did not want to worry Harry with her malady as lately Ed was aware there was something also awry with her. She seemed to be preoccupied with something and was not her usual ebullient self. There was a change in their lovemaking too. Usually, Harry would insist on Ed massaging her breasts and tweaking her nipples but now she kept them hidden under her nightdress explaining to Ed that she had a cold sore and did not want to infect Ed in case it was contagious. Ed had hoped that was the case, a temporary glitch. She missed the foreplay, the rites of their lovemaking which were special to them. After they had been there a few days Harry had pleaded sore feet and exhorted Ed to go by herself to look at some museums and anything else which took her fancy. 'Don't forget the camera,' Harry had called as Ed set off with a map to join the madding crowd. She ventured to the Piazza Navona whose gigantic fountain honoured the four rivers of the earth. She took Harry's camera and took a photo of it then thought she would like a photo of herself beside such a monolithic structure and she asked a woman who acceded to her request. She hoped it would be a good photo. The sun had been in her eyes and she always had a tendency to blink just as the photo was being taken. Well, it is done now she thought putting away the camera to continue walking to the Pantheon. The immensity of the place took her breath away. It was a huge circular edifice, a hallowed place which resembled a church and in which were contained the tombs of famous people such as Raphael and the composer Corelli. She found a seat in one of the pews and cast her eyes up to the apex of the roof, where a circular window was open. Consulting the pamphlet, she had been given she was amazed to learn that the window was constructed to always remain open permitting the air to enter and even the rain. She thought how clever and industrious were those Roman workers to have constructed a place such as this where even outside gigantic pillars had been transported all the way from Egypt. She wished Harry could be here now with her to share this experience. She wondered how she was. She was concerned that something was wrong and wished she would confide in her. Perhaps it was the cocaine which she still insisted on inhaling. She wished she wouldn't. Ed was grateful that she had stopped that habit. Her sleeping had improved and, although there was still the worry of her sexuality, at least she did not have that former anxiety and restlessness. She decided to take some photos and, taking the camera from her bag focused her eye through the lens and clicked the shutter firstly on the roof and then around the walls which were covered in beautiful mosaics. Harry should like these, Ed thought as she slipped the camera back into her bag and made her way outside. After the coolness of the Pantheon the hot air hit her suddenly and she felt slightly dizzy. Across the street she spied a gelato kiosk and made her way there.

'Un bicchiere d'acqua per favore' (a glass of water please) she ordered from the waiter as she sat on one of the chairs under which the overhanging canopy offered a modicum of shade. The water had the desired effect and the dizziness disappeared as fast as it had surfaced. She was still feeling rather hot and had the disinclination to be jostled by the crowds so her decision was to return to Harry and spend what was left of the day with her. They could order a room service late lunch if Harry did not feel up to venturing out. They did that the first day upon their arrival at the hotel. Ed had felt rather decadent reclining on the bed, the two of them in their hotel robes, as the waiter brought in a tray on which was spread an assortment of bruschette and spaghetti cacio e pepe which was just pasta, cheese and pepper, a simple meal but quite delicious. Harry was being so generous towards her insisting on paying for their accommodation and most of their meals leaving Ed rather mystified how Harry could afford it. She had broached the subject over the room service meal but Harry had been rather vague and had mumbled something about a legacy she had been bequeathed by a cousin twice removed. Ed had accepted her explanation but still felt that Harry was not as forthcoming as she could be. She wished she would be more open and confide in her more. After all, Ed had the most to lose in this relationship. She was the one who was leading the double life and she did not really want to lose Tom who hovered in the back of her mind even when she was in the throes of wild passion with Harry. She commenced walking in the direction of the hotel when she felt the need for a toilet. Public conveniences were few but she thought that if she asked politely a restaurant might allow her the use of theirs. If they forbade her, she would purchase a cup of coffee. She walked to the nearest one, the many unoccupied tables signifying a lack of custom.

'Posso usare il tuo bagno?' She asked the waiter who looked down his nose at her making her feel like she was some horrid insect which might infect the establishment.

'Non e per uso pubblico, solo per cliente,' he replied.

It was just as she thought. He was telling her the lavatory was not for public use, only for the customers. She would have to buy a coffee to use the facilities.

'Grazie, una tazza di caffe quindi per favore'. She asked for a cup of coffee and with a flourish the waiter directed her to a table. Just as was turning on his heel, she asked him for the directions to the facilities. After locating them she found the lavatory was not up to her expectations. She had to squat over the bowl as there was no seat on which to sit. As she squatted and relieved herself it resurfaced, the worry which had buried itself under all the layers of her other concerns rearing its ugly head again so that she could no longer avoid it. She inspected her underwear for a sign but still there was nothing. She had not had her monthlies for weeks. But she was never regular and with all the upset in her life she had put it down to that. But, there was also the nausea and lately her breasts were feeling tender. I must be pregnant. God, how will Harry react and Tom? She was always lecturing me about making sure this would not happen, to ensure Tom always use a French letter. It must have been that night in Perthshire when we had drunk too much and Tom had been careless saying that we would be alright and not to worry about anything. She pulled the chain to flush the toilet and returned to the table on which rested the coffee. It tasted bitter and cold matching her mood. She left some lira on the table and made her way back to Harry who would have to be told whatever the outcome or the consequence.

15
CHAPTER

Harry had been rather non plussed when Ed had made her aware of the probable pregnancy. She had expected her lover to make a scene, admonish her for being careless, even suggest ways to rid herself of the problem. However, she had called for coffee to be brought to the room and as they waited for it to arrive she had given a telephone book to Ed. 'Look up numbers for doctors in the area,' she said. Ed did as instructed and passed the telephone to her lover who made a couple of calls in fluent Italian.

'So,' she said somewhat triumphantly placing the receiver back on the cradle 'You have an appointment at 10.00am tomorrow with a Dr Gino Stefano in Via Frattina which is only a block away.'

Ed felt alarmed. Who was this doctor? Was he one of those who terminated unwanted pregnancies?

She asked 'Is he a general practitioner or an obstetrician?'

'I didn't ask, but whoever he is he would be able to confirm if you are pregnant or not.'

That reply did not satisfy Ed. She would have to know what Harry expected her to do.

'Are you coming with me?' Was all she ventured to ask as she could not bring herself to ask anything more she being worried that Harry would demand she terminate this being who may have taken root in her womb.

'Of course, I would not let you go on your own.'

The surly waiter slunk in with the coffee as the diminishing light threw the room into shadow. Harry got up from her chair and turned on the lamp then sat down heavily.

'I haven't asked you about your day.' She said stirring sugar into her drink.

Ed sipped the coffee wishing it had a measure of brandy in it to calm her nerves but she related to Harry all she had seen and the photos she had taken. She asked how Harry had spent her time while she was out enjoying the sights of Rome to be told she had managed to rest and read.

'Do you want to go out to eat tonight or we will order room service?' Asked Harry.

Ed did not feel up to dining in public, being sociable, making conversation. All she wanted was to curl up in bed and wake up to a day free from the worry which was all consuming.

'Oh, I don't feel very hungry actually. You order something for yourself. I think I shall have a bath and an early night.'

Her frazzled psyche was somewhat soothed as she slid under the water scented with a goodly dose of Italian bath salts. She looked down at her breasts to detect any noticeable difference and then down at her stomach which was still flat. But how much longer would it stay that way? How was she going to manage if she was pregnant? Would Harry terminate the relationship or insist she terminate the baby? She lay there for a while letting the water relax her. She closed her eyes and tried not to think about what awaited her tomorrow morning in the doctor's surgery. Then she was aware of a presence in the room. It was Harry holding two glasses of brandy.

'Thought you could do with this.' She said looking down at Ed at her breasts with the dark brown nipples she liked to tease.

'Thanks.' Said Ed disconsolately as she took the glass taking a good mouthful of the amber liquid. It had the desired effect, the warmth sliding down her throat, soothing her perturbation.

Harry quickly drank hers then, just as fast, divested herself of her clothes and climbed into the bath to be with her lover. She sat behind Ed her arms reaching around so she could massage her breasts. Ed was startled at this turn of events as up until now Harry's interest in sex had waned to the point of inactivity.

'I've missed you,' murmured Ed leaning her head back to rest on Harry's shoulder. She wondered if this sexual activity meant that their relationship was safe and she would be there to support her and help her raise this child, if there was a child.

'Let me do the same for you.' Said Ed manoeuvring herself and standing up so she would be behind Harry.

'No, pet.' Said Harry. 'It's alright, just stay there where you are.'

Ed did what Harry wanted and did not question her refusal to have Ed make love to her. Perhaps she still had that cold sore and was embarrassed. There was no more talking, they lay there each with their own thoughts until the water was cold. Then Harry quickly stepped out of the tub and wrapping a towel around her, disappeared into the bedroom. Ed followed soon after and found Harry already in bed.

'Aren't you having any supper either?' Asked Ed throwing her nightdress on and climbing in under the linen sheets.

'I ordered a salad while you were in the bath.'

'Oh, ok.'

Then grasping Harry's hand, she said.

'Harry.'

'Yes, my pet.'

'About my situation.'

'What about it?'

'Well, if I am pregnant, I really don't think I could get rid of it.'

'Nobody is telling you to.'

'So, what are we going to do? I will have to tell Tom. Oh, it's all too much.' Then all her misery burst forth in a flood of tears and she turned away from Harry burying her face in the pillow.

Harry snuggled in beside her and put her arm around her.

She whispered.

'Everything will be sorted in Portovenere my darling. Just wait until then.'

Ed ceased crying when she heard this. What did she mean by that? How would everything be sorted and why would it be sorted in this Portovenere place?

Harry reached over and turned off the lamp.

'Sleep tight.' She said her arms still around Ed.

But Ed could not sleep, she lay awake her mind whirring with worries and questions which would remain unanswered until they arrived in Portovenere. She heard the snores of her lover and wondered how unperturbed she seemed about this situation in which they found themselves. Why did Harry not want Ed to make love to her? They had enjoyed such an uninhibited love life up until now. She then determined she would find out while Harry was asleep, to find out if there really was a cold sore on her breast. She turned towards Harry and lifted the sheet then peeked down her nightdress. Although the light was scant, she could not detect a sore, her breasts were just as they always had been white, pale blue veins snaking under the surface, brown areolas. The mystery deepened. Why was she lying to her? It was dawn when she finally dozed off after tossing and turning all night.

'Rise and shine sleepy head.' Announced Harry, chirpily drawing back the curtains letting the Italian sun into the room.

'It's already 9.00. I ordered breakfast for us.'

'Oh.' Said Ed bleary eyed her hair tousled 'Sorry I overslept but I tossed and turned all night.'

Harry went over and kissed her lips.

'I am sure you will feel better when you have seen this doctor. At least you will know if you are pregnant or not and we can deal with it.'

Ed was unsure about that as she rose from the bed and hurriedly dressed. How were they going to deal with it?

A continental breakfast was wheeled in. It comprised of orange juice, pastries, croissants, parma ham and cheese with a cafetiere of strong coffee. Harry poured the coffee and just as she was placing some ham on a croissant, Ed leapt up and fled to the bathroom where her empty stomach brought forth bile into the lavatory.

'Are you alright in there?' Asked Harry knowing that what Ed had was morning sickness, a definite sign.

Ed thought the same as she wiped her mouth on a piece of toilet paper, her hair stuck to her forehead with the sweat which had formed.

'Yes, thanks I'm coming now.' She called out standing up and splashing water on her flushed face. She pulled the chain and returned to Harry.

'Well, I think we both know what the doctor will say.' Said Harry, wiping her mouth with the napkin and adding cream to the coffee.

Ed knew also. It was morning sickness. There was no other reason.

This was indeed confirmed by the doctor. She was seven weeks pregnant.

They had to check out of the hotel by 1.00pm so they made their way back from the surgery to pack their cases in a leisurely fashion. From Rome they were going by train to Florence as, apart from Portovenere, it was one of Harry's favourite places in Italy. She wanted to show Ed the magnificent Duomo, Michelangelo's statue of David and the Uffizi Gallery. There was so much she wanted her to see but so little time before Portovenere, before Tom would appear and all would be lost. She was glad she had rested in Rome to give her a bit more energy to carry her through. The crowds were always too overwhelming in summer in Rome, Florence was a smaller city and more manageable. She would pace herself for the two days of their stay before their journey to Portovenere. She hoped Ed's nausea would not prevent her from enjoying the rest of their time together and she would be able to put aside her worries about the baby which she had no intention of destroying which was what Harry had suggested.

After three hours aboard the train which had left on time from Stazione Termini they arrived in Florence. Harry summoned a taxi to take them to Via Gino Capponi, to Residenza d'Epoca, which had been an old palace in which Harry had stayed a few years before. It had a room in the attic accessed by a spiral staircase and Harry had booked it just for them.

The taxi stopped at a huge iron door through which they entered with their cases. They walked through a cobblestone courtyard beyond which was a gated private garden Harry telling Ed they would have access to it with a key which they would be given. The key was one of a set which the manager had given to Harry and they were escorted up a spiral staircase to the attic room. Through the window there was a spectacular view. Florence was before them.

'Isn't it wonderful pet?' Enthused Harry her arm around Ed as she pointed out the Duomo, the Uffizi, and the distant hills surrounding the city. It was indeed wonderful, Ed thought as she melded into the arms of her lover in this their room among the rooftops of Florence. She felt different here to how she had felt in Rome. It was hard to explain. Perhaps it had been the hotel which had been rather impersonal with its corridors of rooms and that surly waiter, or was it because she had spent time by herself in that madding crowd not sharing what she had seen with Harry, and no photos taken of the two of them? Perhaps it was the worry of being pregnant which had cast a pall over everything. Now that the pregnancy was confirmed, she had more or less resigned herself to the situation. She forced herself to do as Harry had exhorted, to live now in the moment and trust that all would be settled when they arrived at their destination, Cinque Terre.

They rested for a while then unpacked and descended the spiral stairs out through the courtyard and through the iron door. They walked along the narrow streets to the Duomo with its huge dome and mosaic pavements. It was much cooler inside where they spent time just sitting taking in the splendour, admiring the fifteenth century frescoes of the Last Judgment as well as other works. Ed thought of the Pantheon in Rome, of the open window at the apex and whispered to Harry how she had wished for her to have been there. Harry squeezed her hand sending through her a frisson of happiness. Maybe their relationship would be all right. Harry seemed to be more loving towards her. Last night they had made love with some of the old fervour albeit in the dark Harry permitting Ed to touch one of her breasts. She had asked her again about this but was given the same answer that she still had that sore which Ed now knew to be a lie. However, as Harry had said everything would be settled in Portovenere, she had to cling on to that whatever it meant and just enjoy their time together.

After the Duomo, Harry suggested they have an early supper and an early night as tomorrow they would be visiting the Uffizi which was bound to have hordes of people. They walked a short distance and came across a restaurant whose outside menu looked promising. They went in and due to the early hour found it devoid of customers. They seated themselves near the window which overlooked the Duomo and watched the late afternoon parade sauntering past.

Over veal scallopini and a carafe of sangiovese, they talked about inconsequential matters both skirting around the subject of their relationship and where it was heading. Ed had been reticent to broach the subject not wanting to know what she might hear that Harry would finish with her and exhort her to stay with Tom. She thought of him now as she poked the tiramisu with her spoon. She would soon see him in Portovenere. How would it all pan out? What would happen when he was told about the baby, his baby?

The lagubrious waiter came over to collect the plates noticing Ed's unfinished dessert. He asked if the bella donne had enjoyed the food to which Harry had replied 'Si' handing over the lira. He escorted them to the door adjuring them to call again 'por favor'. They walked back the way they had come and entered the iron door of their palace. They walked over to the gate of the garden. From her bag, Harry took the bunch of keys and located the one which opened the gate. They found themselves in a private oasis filled with the scents of jasmine and roses and various other plants endemic to Italy. Ed was struck with the romance of it and wanted to stay there forever with Harry. She wanted time to stand still and it would be just the two of them without worries or concerns about what would happen in the future. They espied a stone seat tucked away in a mossy corner and in the purple twilight intoxicated by the surroundings, Ed timidly, hesitantly, declared her love for Harry. She had not been able to actually utter the word until now although she had felt it like that time at the cottage in Sussex, and when she was parted from her in the Pantheon. This feeling seemed to come at different times striking her suddenly like a lightning bolt. It was like a force of nature seeking the landscape of her longing, moulding itself to each contour. She felt at this moment she would do anything for her, whatever she asked. She told her this as they sat with hands entwined Ed's head on her lover's shoulder. Harry turned towards her. She cupped her head in her hands and looked into the blue pools of her eyes. She kissed her sweetly. It was like a kiss of gratitude not passion which Ed had been hoping for but felt this would have to suffice. They walked back hand in hand out of the garden and back to their attic room. In each other's arms they cleaved, floating in a dreamless sleep to be washed up onto the shore of the following day.

16
CHAPTER

They were on their way to Portovenere, standing on the deck of the wooden ferry as it plied its way through the inky sea. Portovenere, the place which Harry had said would be the solution to their problems. They passed the cliffs covered with olive groves and grape vines and the tiny fishing villages of Cinque Terre. Rounding the bend jutting out into the sea a craggy cliff came into view and before them was the medieval church of San Pietro. Harry pointed to the grey stone cottage where they would stay which was atop the cave- like grotto dedicated to Byron. It all looked an enchanting place Ed thought, hoping that its magic would be able to wipe away all her perturbation. Tom would soon be arriving, staying with them in the cottage. She did not want to think about that, about the three of them together. It would be like the time in Sussex when she tried to hide evidence of her and Harry's amativeness, ushering Tom out of the cottage to that discomfiting picnic where she did not know where to put herself or what to say.

The ferry pulled up at the wharf. They took their cases and bags of provisions and joined the other few passengers who were being assisted off the boat.

'Do you think you can walk for a while?' Asked Harry, putting down her case and casting her eyes about for some mode of transport.

'Aren't there any vehicles here?' Replied Ed not really feeling like walking. Although her nausea had abated, the sun was hot and there was a blister forming on one of her toes even though she wore sandals.

'No, I'm afraid there aren't pet.' Harry replied. 'It is not like London or Rome.' She also felt hot and her energy was sorely lacking.

'Looks like it is shank's pony for us.' She said picking up her case. 'If we take it slowly, we should be alright.'

Rather put out, Ed picked up her case and the provisions and trudged along behind Harry. She hoped the cottage was close but, remembering the location of it from the ferry, knew it was unlikely and it would also be an uphill climb.

They had not gone very far when a horse and cart pulled up beside them.

'Buongiorno.' Said the moustachioed swarthy faced driver.

'Buongiorno.' They both said in unison hoping that this fellow was their Samaritan come to rescue them from their travails.

He asked them if they wanted a ride and without hesitation, they clambered up into the cart pulling their cases with them.

'Sbalordito,' 'Giddyup.' He shouted and then they were off clopping along through and up the caruggi until they arrived at their destination.

'Grazie, grazie.' They said clambering down from the cart.

'Prego.' He replied doffing his cap. He climbed down from his seat and collecting their cases, placed them at the gate. Before he drove off, Harry asked him if there was someone in the village who could collect them tomorrow to take them into the main part of town.

He had replied that his friend would be able to come at 10.00. Leaving a steaming pile of manure, the horse and his owner clopped back down the way they had come.

'Well, that was fortunate,' said Harry. 'Although I cannot say the same about what that horse left.' 'But,' she added, 'I suppose it will be good for the garden.'

'Just as well he turned up when he did.' Replied Ed. 'I really don't think I would have made it.'

Harry thought the same as they carried their cases to the front door. Last time she had visited, she had come in the winter when it was not hot and the distance did not appear to be as great.

She took the key from her bag and the door creaked open. They went in with the luggage. Ed could not believe how small the cottage was but what it lacked in size it made up for in rustic charm. She loved the old wooden beams and the quietude. Harry went over and opened the shutters letting in the air scented with the sea which was lapping beneath them. She felt weary and was aware of pain in her arm.

'I think I shall lie down for a few minutes before I unpack.' Said Harry making her way into the bedroom. Do you want to have a rest too?'

Ed thought that was a good idea. She could do with a rest in the cool of the cottage so she followed Harry. In the penumbra of the room, they lay on the bed's white linen counterpane. Harry reached over and took Ed's hand in hers. There were no utterances. All was quiet except for the sound of the waves crashing against the rocks beneath them. For a while Ed found the noise soothing but then she felt restless as her thoughts intruded, thoughts about this foetus growing inside her, the coming days and what they would bring. Noticing Harry had dozed off, she got up and crept out of the room. She went outside into the garden which contained hardy shrubs able to withstand the salty air. She noticed a shed to which she walked and opening the creaky door peered inside. Through the gloom and the cobwebs, she discovered a few gardening tools, a rake, secateurs and a shovel. Remembering the pile of manure, she took the shovel and walking out the gate, scooped up the droppings and tossed them underneath a rose bush. It would save Harry doing it and she knew she would be pleased. She put the shovel back into the shed, shut the door then walked out again and over to the cliff.

It was quite a way down to where the roiling sea was dashing against the rocks and she thought of Byron who gamely swam in this inky water, his grotto right underneath her. She supposed Harry had swum in these waters. With whom had she swum? Was it a man or another woman and had they also stayed here in this cottage? She had not told her and Ed had not asked. Maybe I shall ask her while we are here, before Tom arrives. He would be here in two days and what will she say then, will he know that she and Harry are lovers? Her reveries were interrupted by a voice. It was Harry coming towards her.

'Hello pet,' she said. 'I must have dozed off.'

'Yes, you did.' Replied Ed, 'I was restless so I came out to explore a bit. Oh, and I also got rid of that horse's business. I threw it under the rose bush.'

'Did you? That was good of you. Thank you. You saved me dealing with it.'

'It's beautiful, isn't it?' She added moving close to Ed and putting her arm around her shoulders.

They stood there for a few minutes looking out at the sea, Harry pointing to the distant island of Palmaria which she had visited recounting to Ed the delicious fish with lemon and olives she had eaten. Ed thought was this a good time to ask Harry about her previous visits? With whom did she dine on that island? Would she want to know? Before she was able to speak Harry suggested they go for a quick dip before an early supper. The rest had refreshed her somewhat, given her a bit more energy. They returned to the cottage to don their swimming costumes and collect their sunhats Harry deciding at the last moment to take the camera. She closed the door on their luggage which they agreed to unpack upon their return.

Ed followed Harry through the gate and along the cliff path to a rough track which led down to the rocks where they could bathe. It was quite a way down. Ed noticed how slowly Harry was walking but supposed it was because she did not want to slip on the pebbles and the tufts of grass which were under their feet.

'This looks a good place.' Announced Harry. They had arrived at the cluster of rocks from which they would cast themselves into the water. The rock Harry had selected was flatter and smoother than the others.

They settled down on their towels. Ed wanted a photo taken of the two of them on the rock while they were presentable, before the water ruined their hair. She cast her eyes around for someone, anyone who would oblige. She noticed a fisherman not far away on another rock ledge. He was casting a line into the water. She waved to him and pointed to the camera signifying that she would like a photo taken. He nodded and placing his rod down leapt over the rocks to where they were sitting. Agreeing to Ed's request, he took the camera and a photo was taken then he scrambled back to resume his fishing. She was pleased she had a photo of the two of them on this rock by the sea at Portovenere. Tomorrow there might not be time to swim as Harry had planned other activities.

'I think I shall go in.' Said Ed. After the photography session and the hike down the track she felt hotter than ever.

'All right pet,' I will douse myself after you.'

Ed picked her way through the rocks and then threw herself into the water. The shock of its coldness made her gasp. She trod water and looked over at Harry who was waving from the rock. She waved back then struck out with powerful strokes through the water. She ducked under where in the translucence she saw tiny fish darting about. She was now used to the water's chill. It felt refreshing. She wished Harry was swimming with her. She trod water again and signalled for Harry to join her but she was now lying down on the towel with her hat over her eyes. Ed looked over at the grotto of Byron and thought about swimming there but as the sea was smashing into the cave and the tide was becoming higher, she thought better of it. So, she swam back to Harry so that she too could cool off and refresh herself.

'Back so soon?' Harry said raising herself up when she felt Ed's drips of water on her leg.

'Was it nice?'

'Yes. It was freezing at first but then, so refreshing. Are you going in now?' Asked Ed who was wiping off the excess moisture with her towel.

She said she would just slide into the water off the rocks. She had never been much of a swimmer. Not like Ed appeared to be with her breast stroke and freestyle, diving under and over the water like a dolphin. She had reminded her of Edith, the red head who was one of the group who had stayed at the cottage. She had been a wonderful swimmer with a body to match which Harry had taken full advantage of. The relationship had dramatically ended when the husband had discovered them on the lounge in the throes of passion. There was a grand contretemps in the cottage that night as Edith's husband's jealous fists rained down on them both as shouts of 'whores and harlots' resounded around the room. The others, senseless with wine and stoned with cocaine, had been incapable of rendering any assistance. That had been the last time she had seen Edith. She had disappeared from the London scene leaving Harry wondering what had become of her. She had many paramours throughout her life, each with their own attractions. Maddy had been the one who had introduced her to the pleasures of the flesh. Up until the time they had met, she had not conceived of some of the things she had taught her. She thought of Ernest and wondered what had become of him, if he still worked at Fleet Street and if he had met anyone else. He had been alright as far as male lovers were concerned and his money certainly had come in handy. That was not to be denied.

She arose from the towel and placing her hat on the rock, left Ed to dry out in the sun. She made her way carefully to the water. She eased herself in and felt the chill. She clung on to the rock and closed her eyes letting the water wash over her.

'How does that feel?' Cried Ed.

'Lovely,' replied Harry.

She stayed for a few more minutes savouring the coldness then tried to hoist herself up onto the rocks but the pain in her arm prevented her.

She cried out for Ed to assist her explaining as she hoisted her out of the water that she had somehow hurt her arm. As they scrambled across the rocks a cloud obliterated the sun throwing all into shadow and a breeze had appeared cooling the air. They decided to return to the cottage, to put away their clothes and, from their provisions, assemble some sort of early supper with Ed suggesting they eat outside in the garden if it was still warm enough. Tomorrow, Harry planned to show her San Pietro church and Doria castle, also there was a restaurant in the village which was near the wharf and served the most delicious fish pies which Harry knew Ed was partial to. They would lunch there and watch the boats bringing in their catch. They would not see the ferry Tom would be aboard as it was due to arrive at dusk so every moment they had together was precious.

CHAPTER 17

There was nobody there when they entered this hallowed place, the church of San Pietro which Harry had told Ed had been consecrated in 1198. Their eyes had to adjust to the gloom as in the dazzling sun they had walked up and up to the church perched as it was atop the cliff. Harry had been grateful to have arrived and to sit down in one of the pews out of the heat. Their conveyance had arrived punctually at 10.00 the time Harry had stipulated and they had been transported nearby to the location of Doria Castle. Then a climb had to be undertaken as the castle was also at the apex of a cliff. Harry hoped it was not too much for Ed, all this walking about in the heat but she was determined to show her and share with her all these wondrous sights before Tom arrived. It was amongst the ruins of the castle where they had sat on the grass looking down towards the gulf of poets that Ed had summoned the courage to ask her lover had she stayed with someone else in the cottage here, in Portovenere. Harry took Ed's hand and put it to her lips. She told her she had stayed in the cottage with a group from London. She did not tell her how risqué they were, about her dalliance with Edith nor about the bruises she had suffered from Edith's husband's fists. Ed seemed content with Harry's answer. She preferred not to know any more information, information which would kill this fantasy she had that Ed was Harry's only true love, the only one she called 'pet'. Last night in bed she had even called her 'darling' after tenderly making love to her. She had never called her that in the past, not even in their attic room in Florence, after Ed had bared her soul in the garden and told her she loved her. She looked now across at Harry. She seemed to be wincing and rubbing the top of her arm towards her breast.

'Is your arm still sore?' She asked.

'Yes, I cannot think what I did to it, maybe it was when I got off the cart. I must have bumped it or something.'

Their attention was then diverted by a peregrine falcon. They watched as it soared across the sky and over the gulf. To be a bird like that Ed mused, flying free in the sky completely devoid of worries or concerns about relationships, about giving birth. She put her hand on her stomach which did not feel as flat as before and lately she had detected a slight fluttering sensation like a butterfly's wings. It must be the baby moving she had thought, but she did not want it. However, at the same time she did not want to be rid of it either. She was in such a quandary about the whole business.

'Absorbed with the view?' Asked Harry moving closer to her so their shoulders touched.

'Yes, and about the baby,' she replied pulling a dandelion from the grass. She puffed at it and its spores blew away on the air.

Harry took her hand and tucked a stray tendril behind Ed's ear. She was cognisant of her quandary and concern but was reluctant to say anything which might raise her hopes that they would be a family.

She said.

'Tom will be here later and I'm sure when you tell him he will be thrilled at the news.'

Ed was unsure about that. Did that mean Harry wanted her to be with him and raise this child she was carrying? She did not know much about babies only they dirtied nappies which had to be washed and they cried a lot and made a mess.

Harry interrupted her thoughts then, thoughts from which she was glad to be rescued.

'I think we should go now pet,' she said easing herself off the grass. 'I want to show you San Pietro before we have lunch.'

They made their way down from the castle on the cliff and walked in the direction of the church.

'Let's light some candles,' whispered Harry after they had sat for a while in the pew relishing the gloom and the cool of the nave. They made their way to the altar in front of which candles flickered. They took two, lit them and placed them in the sconces. They knelt together on the small kneeler and only God was privy to their prayers. He heard that Ed wanted Him to tell her what to do about her relationship with Harry and with Tom and to make everything all right about the baby she was carrying. He heard Harry asking for His forgiveness for all her past transgressions and to give her courage to deal with whatever lay ahead.

Harry wanted to take Ed outside right to the top of the church, to show her the magnificent view. However, there were steep steps and she was concerned about Ed who was already wilting in the heat so she abandoned that idea. Anyway, she thought, the castle's view had been just as good. They made their way out of the church and down to the track where a cart was waiting to take them to the cafe which Harry had suggested.

Inside in the relative cool over fish pies and a carafe of chianti, the conversation revolved around the day's activities, Harry wanting to know what Ed thought of this place, if it held the same fascination as it did for her, San Pietro, Doria Castle, Byron's grotto, all those places which Harry held dear.

'Oh yes, yes, Harry I love it all,' she had enthused eyes aglow with fervour taking her lover's hand across the table.

Harry felt then a frisson of happiness. It was what she wanted to hear that Ed shared the same love for Portovenere as she had.

'And,' Ed added, 'I wish we could stay longer and I would not have to go back to old Teesdale with his moustache full of food.'

Then another idea formed.

'Maybe we can come back here again one day, just the two of us and relive our memories.'

As the words left her mouth, she knew somehow that would not happen. There was the child to consider and Tom entered the equation. This was probably the last time they would both be here.

Harry thoughts were the same. This meal would be like their last supper. Instead of bread, it was fish pies.

They sipped their wine and looked about them, at the weathered Cinque Terre women and the fishermen tending their boats, bringing in their catch. Ed looked over at the wharf where Tom was due to alight from the ferry which would leave Riomaggiore at 5.30. Harry had insisted that Ed be there to meet him, to have some supper with him, to discuss pertinent matters before bringing him back to the cottage. Ed felt uneasy about that. She would rather Harry be there with her to be the bulwark of the awkwardness she would feel. The thought of having a tete a tete supper with Tom, apprising him of their Italian sojourn and of the baby seemed all too much to contemplate.

Harry consulted her watch. It was time for them to leave and return to the cottage on the cliff. She paid the bill and Ed followed her outside. The heat had abated somewhat and there was a slight breeze ruffling the water. Harry signalled a cart and then they were on their way clopping through the caruggi and up to the cottage. Ed thought she would miss hopping into and out of these carts. She felt they were more relaxing than the motor vehicles with their noisy crankshafts and bellowing horns. She would be soon in another cart to be taken to the wharf to meet Tom. As soon as they arrived at the cottage, she would try to persuade Harry to come with her.

However, Harry had pleaded a headache and fatigue after their outing in the heat. She made up the lounge and told Ed she was going to retire early.

'But why are you sleeping here, on this?' Ed asked waving her hand at the lounge which was now covered with a pillow and a sheet.

'Because my love,' she had replied, 'you and Tom will be sharing the bed.'

Ed had wondered about the sleeping arrangements. She supposed it would have looked too suspicious if she and Harry shared the double bed and Tom was relegated to the lounge. But, as in other matters regarding this risqué relationship she had chosen to ignore the realities, had put her head in the sand pretending everything would resolve but, in her heart, knew it would not.

Ed left Harry on the lounge and went into the bathroom to run a bath. It had been a long day walking about in the heat and she still had the evening to negotiate. She caught a glimpse of herself in the mirror, her nose was reddened by the sun and she felt sticky with perspiration. She studied her face. What did she really look like she wondered? Her mother's eyes and hair, of course, something of her father in her nose, not much she could see of her grandparents. What did it all add up to? How much choice did she have in how she spoke, acted, loved. Was there someone in her family who had made her mistakes, was it stamped into her genes? She eased herself into the tub and let the warm water wash over her. She took the soap and flayed the flannel over her face and around her neck wondering what dress she would wear tonight. Harry liked the white sundress with the red polka dots, always saying it showed her shoulders to advantage. She liked Harry to see her looking her best, always ensuring there was no lipstick on her teeth and her hair was tidy. If her breath was fresh and her stocking seams were straight. Did she feel this way with Tom? Did she or had she cared what he had thought of her appearance? She had not taken well to any criticisms he had occasionally flung at her such as her penchant for leaving wet bath towels on the floor and her clothes not hung up properly in the wardrobe. Was this a sign of her true feelings? Was she in love with Harry and not Tom?

'You look lovely pet,' said Harry from the lounge on which she was reclining.

Ed had decided to wear the sundress Harry preferred and had covered her nose with powder.

She moved her shoulders this way and that to show them off to Harry. She knew that they looked nice, gleaming and tanned by the Italian sun.

'Tom should approve,' added Harry.

It was time to go. Ed had arranged to be collected by the cart at 5.45 and it was now nearly that time.

She walked over to Harry to give her a farewell kiss but Harry pulled her down on the lounge enveloping her in a hug.

'Goodbye my pet,' she said after their lips had mingled.

'Have a lovely time with Tom and don't rush back, as I said I am having an early night.'

Ed walked to the door. She waved at Harry then walked out into the dusk and through the gate. She climbed aboard the cart which would take her to the wharf where Tom would be waiting.

18
CHAPTER

While Harry and Ed had been enjoying their holiday, Ernest had been occupied filing reports on the festival in Sienna. However, the newspaper's budget was limited in how much they allocated to journalists' overseas assignments, so Ernest found himself in an insalubrious hotel in one of the narrow lanes a few blocks from the Piazza del Campo. His tiny room accessed by six flights of stairs reminded him of a garret tucked away at the top of the building. Sparsely furnished with an iron bed, a drunken wardrobe and a table with a lamp which worked intermittently, there was hardly room to move. The small window afforded a view of a grey roof immersed in pigeon droppings and butts of cigarettes which he surmised was probably from a previous guest driven to exasperation by his surroundings. He had to complain to the manager about the lamp as he needed all the light he could muster to type his reports but that was met by a shrug of the shoulders and a vague promise for someone to repair it.

'Bloody stingy of the office to put me in this joint' he railed as the lamp turned off once again when he was half down the page. He wondered what Jim would have thought of it, poor old Jim recovering in hospital from post operative complications. Ernest determined he would find better accommodation, even putting his own money towards the cost. He had won quite a bit of lira on the winning horse so he could afford a more decent place and had wasted no time ensconcing himself in more expensive restaurants. It was at one of these dining establishments, 'Picolo' around the corner from the cathedral, that he found himself buying a Campari and soda at the bar for a rather attractive woman. With her blonde shingled hair and blood lipstick she had reminded him of Harriette. Her name was Giovanna but, unlike Harriette, her personality was ebullient albeit tempered with mournful eyes. This, she had told him in passable English was because her husband had left her for another woman. Ernest sympathised with her. He knew what it was like to be thrown over and cast aside for another woman as he had. After ordering another round of Camparis, sans soda, Ernest invited her to join him for dinner. He felt somewhat of an affinity with her. Over antipasto, Ernest's phrase book was feverishly consulted as he tried to follow what she was saying as she lurched from English to Italian depending how upset she felt. There were lots of 'mama mias' and 'testa di cazzo' meaning her husband was a dickhead and 'puttana' his huzzy was a bitch. After a few glasses of Merlot which Ernest had ordered she became more voluble as her hands gesticulated to emphasise the points. He looked around to see if they were attracting attention but the diners were too busy eating and also conversing in a raucous manner. These Italians certainly know how to vent their emotions, thought Ernest as he stabbed his piece of rare steak releasing the blood which leaked onto his plate. In England, all eyes would be swivelling at the slightest sign of raised voices, especially in a restaurant of this calibre. Not in Italy though. It was refreshing. He wanted to tell her what he thought of Harriette. He already knew the word for bitch. He looked up the word for lesbian. It was lesbica. So, when Giovanna's tirade had settled to a trickle and she was busy winding spaghetti onto her fork, Ernest attempted to tell her his girlfriend had been a lesbica puttana. Her eyes widened and with a strand of spaghetti half way to her mouth she collapsed in laughter. 'Lesbica?' She cried in astonishment.

'Si, lesbica' replied Ernest who now also was seeing the humour of it and could hardly believe what he had uttered in such a public place.

'Lesbica puttana!' he shouted again uncaring who heard him. It felt good. It was rather cathartic. He could never do this in England. Not even in those Fleet Street traps which he frequented. He wished Harriette was here now. He would have loved to tell her to her face that she was a lesbica puttana. Then the two of them were both laughing and he thought how good it felt. It was a long time since he laughed like this, a good belly laugh which brought a tear to the eye and a shortness of breath. This is what was meant by la dolce vita. He certainly could do with more of it. It was when the tiramisu was finished Giovanna invited him to her place, for a coffee capisce? Ernest understood about the coffee, but he was unsure that is all he might be wanting. Giovanna was certainly attractive and had a good figure as well. That husband of hers did not know when he had it so good and he wondered how his new lover measured up. He could not imagine she could be better looking than Giovanna.

He peeled off the lira from his stash and left it on the table for the maitre'd who came bustling over to escort them out the door. It was a short walk from the restaurant to Giovanna's chic apartment. Amidst the gilt lamps and plush furnishings, Ernest was plied with brandy. He awoke to find himself not in his garret, but on the lounge covered with a counterpane as the aroma of strong Italian coffee wafted in from the kitchen.

'Buongiorno, good morning,' said Giovanna as she wandered in garbed in a couture dress with lipstick to match, a heady perfume trailing in her wake. She was carrying a tray of mugs of coffee and a plate of bread rolls with jam. He wondered where she would be going this early all dressed up like that.

Ernest sat up. His mouth felt like the bottom of a birdcage. He must have really overdone it last night.

'Buongiorno,' he sheepishly replied.

He indicated he wanted to use the bathroom.

'Si,' Giovanna said pointing to its location.

He scuttled off to relieve himself and splash his face with water. Then he stuck his head under the tap to slake his thirst. Looking in the mirror, he was horrified at the vision which greeted him. He was in need of a shave and his eyes were rheumy. He could not remember how much he had drunk last night nor could he remember if he had sex with Giovanna. He supposed he had not as he would have woken up in her bed and not on the lounge but, maybe they had done it on the lounge. It was a complete blank. He dried his face on one of the fluffy towels and returned to the lounge room where Giovanna was sitting waiting for him.

He sat down next to her. He did not know whether to ask her if they had sex. He felt at a disadvantage sitting there in his crumpled clothes, his unshaven face, so he decided to say nothing. Instead, he took a good swig of coffee and bit into a roll. The coffee was just what he needed. Good and strong. It made him feel more human.

She patted his knee then and enquired how he felt. If he had slept or not to which he mumbled, 'Si, grazie' while wiping some jam from his fingers with the linen napkin provided. He took another sip of coffee then managed to ask her what they had talked about last night in the hope she might divulge if they had been intimate. Wiping her mouth delicately and putting down her coffee on the small gleaming table, she replied that he told her he was a reporter from England covering the horse race, he was staying in a shit hotel with a shit lamp and there was birds' shit on the roof. She told him he seemed to like the word shit. He had drunk a lot of brandy and was unfit to walk back to his accommodation so she allowed him to sleep on the lounge. There was no mention of anything else occurring so Ernest assumed he had a celibate night. He conveyed his thanks and said when he finished breakfast, he would return to his hotel to freshen up and then look for better accommodation.

'Alora, you stay here no?'

'Here, with you?'

'Si, plenty of room,' she said waving her hand around indicating the spaciousness of their surroundings. It was certainly a huge apartment and he noticed there was a balcony off this room. It would no doubt have a superb view of Sienna.

Ernest was unsure if he should accept her offer. Had her husband really deserted her or was he likely to come storming in to the apartment and stab him in the back? He had heard there were Italians like that, jealous, hot blooded and what if he is involved with the mafia? This apartment exuded wealth and it might have been because of ill-gotten gains.

He asked.

'What does your husband do? Has he moved out?'

'He is chief of carabinieri,' she replied. Then with a disdainful look. 'He is living with that puttana.'

'And he won't be visiting you?'

'No, no, I changed locks.'

Ernest still was not convinced. If this fellow was the commissioner of police he could easily pick the lock and maybe arrest Ernest in the process.

'I go to avvocato this morning.'

'Avvocato?'

'Lawyer.'

'Ah, so you get divorce?'

'Si.'

That was why she was dressed so smartly. She had an appointment with a lawyer. He thought about his options. It would save him looking around for another place as he was planning only to stay in Sienna for another couple of days now that the race was over. Then he planned to use the rest of his holidays visiting Pisa. He always wanted to see that leaning tower, to have his photo taken trying to hold it up like every other tourist before him. He had taken numerous photos. Firstly, the Trevi fountain and the Spanish steps in Rome where he ate the most delicious gelato, then at the festival, of the horses racing around the track, the people in the bleachers.

He knew Herbie, his brother would love to look at those as he had a fondness for horses and would have loved to ride them only his disability prevented it. He would have loved being here and seeing the horses and the jockeys in their bright colours, the people cheering and waving. He described it all to him in a letter which he managed to write in between the moods of the lamp.

Dear Herbie,

I thought I would write you a few lines as I know how much you enjoy reading letters. However, by the time you receive this I will probably be home with the photos for you and mother to look at.

The flight to Rome was rather rough and it was quite cold in the cabin necessitating me to wind a scarf around my neck but I soon warmed up when I walked out of the terminal and felt that hot Roman sun beating down.

Rome was busy. Full of summer tourists and I joined them at the Trevi Fountain and the Spanish Steps where I had the most delicious gelato. You would have loved it as it was your favourite flavour, lemon.

Now I am in Sienna covering this unique horse festival and it would have to be seen to be believed. The race is over four days and the city is divided into areas or contrade. Each contrada has its own emblem and colours and there are flags and emblems displayed along the streets, just like street signs. The start is in the "mossa," an area set up in the piazza and as the space is small, the horses are right next to each other and must run three laps around the Campo. The first horse to cross the finish line even if it does not have a jockey wins the race and receives what is called the Drapellone. You might be pleased to know that I wagered a few bets and my horse won!

I am planning to visit Pisa in a couple of days and will take some photos of me trying to stop that tower from falling ha ha.

Hope you and mother are well and I look forward to seeing you both when I return to Blighty.

Take care of yourself and mother
Your loving brother
Ernie

He hoped they would enjoy hearing from him about his visit abroad, his poor widowed mother and disabled brother. He hated to think of them both stuck in that coal miner's cottage in Tyldesley with only pensions to live on. He determined if he ever found himself with extra funds he would do all he could to obtain better accommodation for them, make their lives more comfortable. He had broached the subject once with his mother but her reply had been that she was used to living there. It was where she had lived all her married life. It was where she had given birth to Ernest and Herbie, she had her neighbours whom she had known all these years and she would not know how to live anywhere else.

'Grazie, Giovanna,' Ernest suddenly said having made up his mind, 'if you think it is ok I will accept your kind offer but I will only stay for two days as I am going to Pisa.'

'To see tower, no?' She replied smiling.

'Si, yes, the tower.'

She placed the mugs and plates on the tray and proceeded to the kitchen, her heels clicking on the black and white tiled floor. Ernest busied himself folding up the counterpane and placing it on the lounge. He straightened the cushions wondering as he did so if he would be sleeping in her bed for the two nights or be relegated to the second bedroom which he had noticed on his way back from the bathroom.

Giovanna returned with her handbag. She told him she would be back about 12.15 and he could bring his luggage around then. They left the apartment, he to check out of the hotel and she to consult with the avvocato.

After changing his clothes and making himself presentable, he took pleasure in leaving the garret, the dodgy lamp and the shit view as he paid the manager what he owed. He felt inclined to deduct a few lira to compensate for the inconvenience of the bad lighting but it was the office who was paying not him and the tariff was cheap enough. He left his luggage in a storeroom then made his way to the cathedral which up until now he had not had the opportunity to see. It was like many cathedrals he had visited, nothing out of the ordinary, gloomy, waxy air. However, at least it was a chance to escape the heat for a little while, so he sat in one of the pews to gather his thoughts. He supposed he should take Giovanna to lunch for allowing him to stay even though he had funded her dinner and drinks last night. He had certainly enjoyed himself at that restaurant and still was in disbelief that he had actually shouted out that Harriette was a lesbian bitch. He wondered who she was with now and if she was still wheedling for money. He had been a mug to have been taken in by her, funding her extravagances, he should have got shot of her long before he did. But that was in the past and this was the present and he had Pisa to look forward to and two nights at Giovanna's.

He exited the cathedral and wandered aimlessly around the cobblestone streets, looking in shop windows, admiring the euchre-coloured buildings still festooned with the flags and emblems of the horse festival. He passed by a restaurant which had an outdoor area and decided that was where he would have lunch with Giovanna. He enjoyed eating alfresco whenever he could which was not often as, even in summer, it was usually too cloudy and not very warm but here today, in Italy, the sun was shining and there was not a cloud in the sky. He entered the restaurant and made a booking for 12.30pm. It was now 11.30 and he was due back at Giovanna's with his luggage at 12.15. He felt like another coffee. He had only managed one at Giovanna's which in his untidy state had been drunk with a modicum of self-consciousness. He noticed a hole in the wall place where a gaggle of besuited men stood about downing espressos. He pushed his way to the counter and placed his order musing how Italians preferred to drink their coffee standing up rather than sitting down in comfort. Espresso now in hand, he stood with these customers feeling like one of them but knowing he was not. He was just a chap from England here on a working holiday. As their loquacity drifted around him, he wished he had a greater knowledge of the language and not just the basics. He discerned a few words here and there. It seemed they had gripes about the government and the economy not unlike what people were complaining about at home. He thought people were basically the same. Their concerns seemed to be about the government, how they should be doing more, about money and if they had enough to pay the bills and feed their families. He finished the rest of the coffee, left the debate and wandered back to Giovanna's apartment.

19
CHAPTER

Tom had found her in a foetal position on the floor by the lounge, the room reverberating with the sounds of an animal in pain. They had returned from the restaurant where Edwina had given him the news, the news that she was pregnant, was having his baby. His joy was bountiful. There was a marriage proposal and a bottle of champagne had been ordered in celebration, but she was unsure. In silence they had travelled back to the cottage in the cart from which Edwina had hastily leapt to tell Harriette what had transpired leaving Tom extracting his luggage from the cart and sorting out the fare. Edwina had found the cottage in darkness.

'Harry, Harry where are you?' She had shouted running from room to room but there was no reply. The cottage was empty. There was no sign of her lover only a note left for her on the pillow on the lounge. It was that note which had unravelled her taking away her breath and desire for living. Before she dissolved completely, before Tom came in, she hid the note stuffing it down the front of her dress, the dress which her lover had liked best. Tom would never read what she wrote, nor would anyone else. Then she lay on the floor and entered a world, a cold world devoid of her Harry, her beloved. She had felt Tom's hands and his arms around her as he tried to coax from her what was wrong. Alarmed at what he heard, he had run outside to see if the driver was still there and had shouted to his retreating back to send for the carabineri. Swiftly they arrived on horseback from the village and Edwina had been questioned after Tom had persuaded her to take a little brandy to calm her nerves, to make her more coherent. Through the fog of despair and grief, she tried to answer their questions which were written down by one of them with a pencil in a notebook. She told them Harriette was missing and she thought she had fallen over the cliff. She told them that she liked to take a walk in the evening along the cliff, to hear the sea crashing against and into Byron's grotto. There was then a stampede to the cliff down which torches were flashed but there was nothing to see, nothing but the inky blackness of the Ligurian sea dashing against the rocks.

The carabineri had asked Tom if he wished to stay the night in the cottage with Edwina as tomorrow, they would have to leave Portovenere and go to Sienna which was the nearest main city where a formal interview would be conducted and statements obtained. A cart would come and transport them and their luggage to the wharf for the 9.15am ferry to Riomaggiore, from whence they would board a train.

He thought it was too late to find other accommodation in the village so had coaxed her into bed, the bed which Edwina and Harriette had shared, where they had cleaved to each other, where her lover had called her 'pet. She would never be called that again. Tom tried his best to comfort her but she pulled away from him and curled up into herself saturating the pillow with her tears. He lay there listening to the sea, the sea which must have claimed Harriette. In his heart he knew they must have been more than friends for Edwina to have been so stricken. Only a lover would manifest so great a grief. He thought and hoped that time would heal her, that this baby which was his would be the salve for her wound and bind them together. He would provide for her, they would live in a nice house, near the sea if that was what she wanted, perhaps somewhere like Cornwall. He could establish a practice in one of those villages or even work as an employee. He would even try to turn a blind eye to her untidiness, let her leave her wet towels on the floor and her books askew on the shelf. He did not care if her drawers were a mad jumble of socks, stockings and camisoles all vying for space. She could even have her music on while he did his crossword as long as she was his wife and a mother to his child.

After that terrible night, Tom packed Edwina's things leaving anything belonging to Harriette in the cottage as the authorities had suggested. He was keen to obtain some medical assistance as Edwina's trance like state was quite worrying. She moved like an automaton, her eyes glazed, sitting in the cart then aboard the ferry with nary a word spoken. All he could do was hold her hand, squeeze it occasionally to let her know he was trying to offer her solace, some sort of support in her time of need.

He had asked one of the deckhands if he knew of a doctor in Riomaggiore. He was directed to a location which he was told was up one of the steep caruggi and would take about 20 minutes. Tom estimated that would mean 40 minutes there and back and combined with the consultation he should allow an hour. He knew the train would not arrive for another hour and a half so they would just have time. They walked to the train station to store their luggage, Tom carrying their cases as Edwina trailed along behind him. He wished she would walk a bit faster but knew she could not. Her fragile condition, her pregnancy and the heat of the day all conspired to prevent it. They arrived at the station and Tom stored the luggage glad to be free of it, his arms were aching and he was perspiring profusely even though his sleeves were rolled up and he was wearing a panama hat. Edwina was still dressed in the polka dot sundress she had worn the night he had arrived. She had worn it to bed not wanting to remove it. She did not care about the state of it, creased and wrinkled. She seemed to have an attachment to it as though it would bring her closer to Harriette.

Unencumbered, they commenced walking up the caruggi to the doctor's residence as Tom hoped and prayed that the physician would be there. No words emanated from Edwina's mouth, it was clamped, shutting in all her sorrow and despair. She allowed Tom to take her elbow, to assist her up the incline but she did not feel comforted by that, it was just a support, something akin to a walking stick or similar.

Finally, they arrived at their destination. Tom looked around trying to see a sign on a house indicating, 'medico' but there was nothing to indicate a doctor's residence. An old woman came shuffling towards them, garbed in black, she was carrying a dowager's hump and a string bag of onions.

'Buongiorno,' Tom exclaimedm. 'Dove il dottore por favor?' 'Where is doctor please?' he asked.

'Alora,' she said then indicated with a bony finger to a house across the street.

'Grazie,' said Tom while Edwina stood beside him her eyes still blank.

He took her elbow and walked her across the road to the house which he hoped contained medical assistance. He rang the bell and what seemed an inordinate amount of time but was probably only a minute, the door was opened by a bespectacled bearded man of advancing years.

'Si,' he said.

'Buongiorno,' replied Tom, 'Sei un dottore?'

'Si.'

He ushered them in and bade them sit down as Tom related all of Edwina's maladies, her pregnancy, the supposed drowning of her best friend which led to the state she was now in. He told him they were catching a train in about half an hour to Sienna where they had an appointment with the carabinieri.

The doctor took his stethoscope, listened to her heart, looked into her eyes and asked her questions to which he received no reply. He felt her pulse then stroking his beard, told Tom she would need a sedative to tide her over until they reached Sienna and more medical help could be given. He took a pen and dipping it into the ink well wrote a letter which he told Tom to hand over to the next dottore. Then he arose from his chair and walked over to an array of bottles and jars. From one of these he poured a white liquid into a medicine glass and brought it over to Edwina. He put it to her lips and coaxed her to drink it.

The consultation was over and after Tom had paid the doctor what he was owed he helped Edwina from the chair and guided her to the door.

'Aspettare,' 'wait,' said the doctor.

He said he would drive them to the station as Edwina was in no condition to undertake another long walk in the sun. So, it was another cart in which they travelled, the horse clopping down the steep caruggi they had previously negotiated. What a kind doctor he was Tom thought, to see us without an appointment and then to drive us to the station. He had been concerned about Edwina undertaking another walk in the heat and had even envisaged carrying her.

The train arrived on time, the doctor seeing them off safely telling Tom that Edwina would probably sleep during the journey but to keep an eye on her as well. He had provided Tom with a bottle of water and advised that Edwina must try to drink some to prevent dehydration.

Edwina had slept for most of the journey her head cradled in Tom's accommodating lap as the train steamed its way through tunnels and along the cliffs until their arrival in Sienna. Now and then he managed to trickle some water between her lips, reluctant to wake her as he was unsure how she would react, if she would still be in that zombie like state as before. He thought he would rather her be crying or yelling, anything but that silence which seemed to chill him to the core.

'Where are we?' She murmured rubbing her eyes as the train jolted into the station and she saw Tom beside her in the train compartment.

'In Sienna' he replied then, 'how do you feel?'

'I don't know. I feel strange like I have been sleeping forever. Why are we here in Sienna?'

'We have things to take care of, dearest.'

He dared not mention anything about seeing the carabineri, it would lead to other things, things he did not want her to remember, not yet anyway, not until they were there.

He pulled their cases from the rack and guided her off the train. Although the doctor advised Edwina to see another doctor when they arrived, Tom thought they should present themselves at the carabineri headquarters first. She seemed better than before, and at least she was speaking although vague and her memory somewhat impaired. After receiving directions from the station master, they set off to the place where he and Edwina would again be interviewed and their statements taken regarding the missing person, Harriette Cavendish.

While they were making their way to headquarters, Ernest had already arrived with his notebook and pencil to get a scoop for the Daily Mail delaying his trip to Pisa. He had stayed two nights with Giovanna. They had lunched and dined and in her large bed of satin sheets they had drunk wine, made wild, mad passionate love, laughed and joked about her dickhead husband and his lesbica. She had met her ex-husband at the lawyers' conference as the terms of the divorce were negotiated. He however, had to leave before a settlement was reached as word had come that an English woman was missing, believed drowned in Portovenere and he was needed at the office. Giovanna had conveyed this news to Ernest as she knew he was a journalist and would be interested in reporting on a presumed drowned English woman. He had wondered who she was, was she someone of whom he knew, one of the London crowd who usually caroused around the continent?

He had been told by one of the carabineri to wait in an annex until the superintendent was ready to see him, after the interview with the witnesses had concluded. He sat on one of the hard chairs, lit a cigarette and looked about him. It was a rather dismal room, green linoed floor, grey walls, peeling paint. He blew smoke up into the air which circled around the picture of Mussolini who stared down at him. At home it would have been a picture of King George V. He thought the King looked better than this Mussolini chap who had rather a fat and pompous visage. He took another drag of his cigarette and thought about this scoop he would be making for the newspaper. There would not be many reporters over here from Britain as most of them would have returned after the festival and there would not be many who would have had the inside information as he had. If he had not met Giovanna, the ex-wife of the commissioner of police, he would have been as ignorant as anyone else. He lit another cigarette and thought about her. Was she just having a bit of fun, a bit of sex to spite her husband? He did not know, he only knew that he felt so alive in her company with her joie de vivre, her zest for life, even in the throes of a divorce. She had indicated that she would come with him to Pisa, laughing that they together could hold up that tower. It was certainly tempting and he would have someone with whom to go, someone who spoke fluent Italian. His reverie was interrupted. A small bald man in a uniform strode in. He introduced himself as superintendent and Ernest was to follow him, por favore, into another room where his questions would be answered. He would have liked to question the commissioner, to see what he looked like, if he resembled a Mafioso but then, he thought, they would look like average people, they would not sport horns on their heads or breathe fire.

Making their way along a corridor, they passed two people who he presumed were the witnesses. The woman looked as though she had been through a wringer, hair askew, wrinkled dress, swollen red eyes hanging on to the arm of the fellow who hurried her along wanting to be out of this place and on their way.

Ernest and the superintendent entered the room. It was not unlike the room he had previously been in however, there was a mercury vapour lamp protruding from the ceiling and there was a distinct odour of tobacco. Ernest pulled out a chair sitting opposite the superintendent. He took out his notebook and with pencil poised, wrote down what the superintendent was telling him albeit in broken English. Edwina Banks, Tom's fiancé had been holidaying with the missing woman in Italy. They had been staying in a cottage on a cliff in Portovenere. Tom had arrived by ferry and Edwina had met him. They had gone for dinner and when they had returned to the cottage Edwina had discovered that her friend was missing and had probably fallen over the cliff where she liked to walk in the evening. The police had been notified and searches had been conducted but there had been no sign of a body. It was presumed that a drowning had taken place and her body had been swept out to sea.

Ernest sat back and put the pencil behind his ear. He cast his eye over what he had written and he then asked for Tom's and Edwina's full names. It was when he had asked the name of the missing woman he felt the shock and he found it hard to write: Cavendish, Harriette Cavendish. He was in disbelief that it was her and then he knew, he knew that the distraught woman he had passed in the corridor was certain to be Harriette's latest lover. He had not recognised her. She did not appear to be one of that louche London crowd with which Harriette had consorted. He wondered if this chap Tom knew what his fiancé had been up to, that she was bi sexual or had he been hoodwinked. However, it was none of his business. He was here to write the report and he could not wait to send it off. What a stir it would cause. Harriette Cavendish, the daughter of that minister, drowned in Italy. Had she drowned or committed suicide? She had probably been snorting cocaine as was her habit. He could not imagine she would have given that up however, if her body was found, there would be an autopsy and all would be revealed. He thanked the superintendent for his time then departed to scuttle off to Giovanna's apartment where in good light he typed:

Sienna, Italy

Ernest Blackman

Harriette Cavendish, the daughter of the Labour Minister, Anthony Cavendish, is missing presumed drowned in Portovenere, a village in the Cinque Terre area in northern Italy.

Her friend, Edwina Banks, with whom she had been holidaying had stated that she assumed her friend had fallen to her death off the cliff. A search has been conducted but a body has not been found. An investigation has been commenced but at this time the opinion of the authorities is that the death was accidental.

He pulled the sheet of paper from the typewriter and rushed to the post office where his report would wing its way to the Daily Mail giving Londoners more than their marmalade and toast to digest in the morning.

CHAPTER 20

1986

Aunt's funeral had been held a couple of weeks after the autopsy which revealed she had died from complications due to pneumonia thereby exonerating the Filipino nurse. However, I still retained suspicions about her that she meant to do harm to my aunt, but as nothing was proven she had been free to go about her business. I had inserted aunt's death notice in the paper as I had been unable to locate a list of her friends/acquaintances but thankfully they had seen it and had attended bearing flowers and perhaps curiosity more than sadness. There had been nothing sent from her son so deep was their estrangement. I felt rather sorry as he was her only child. There were a few smirks and raised eyebrows when, 'Nothing Like a Dame,' reverberated through the chapel at the conclusion of the service everyone exclaiming at the pub wake how appropriate the song was. I had the impression that those in attendance were all aware of her feistiness and bombast.

Over the sherry and ale, there was a good deal of chatter about the manner of her demise and I found myself more than once being asked for my opinion. 'Do you think that nurse really tried to kill her dear?' I was relieved when they all departed having had their fill of the repast and had been grateful for Margo's company albeit for a short time, as she had to collect her son from school. I had relayed my suspicions to her about that nurse but she thought I was being rather paranoid about the episode. 'After all Georgia,' she said, 'The legal system said she had not had a case to answer so just forget about it. Your aunt died from natural causes.' I tried to do as she had said to put it all behind me and move on but deep in the crevice of my mind there still lurked the thought the nurse was not as innocent as she was portrayed. However, there was something else which soon overtook me, something rather unexpected. It was in the form of a telephone call from aunt's solicitor, Mr Cowdrey who requested that I present myself at his office to discuss aunt's will. To my astonishment, I had been made the main beneficiary of her estate with the balance going to the Cat Protection Society of which aunt had been a patron. I could scarcely believe it. I had inherited her residence in Marylebone Road! It would be worth a sizeable sum if it was put on the market and in the meantime I could either move in and relinquish my flat or rent out aunt's place and receive a good return. I had immediately contacted Margo screaming through the phone that I was now a lady of means and we had met for cocktails and dinner, she prevailing upon her husband to mind Hamish while we celebrated and discussed my pecuniary interests.

'You know,' I said to Margo twirling the little umbrella which was in my margarita. 'I always had a hankering to open a little bookshop which sells coffee, where people can read and hang out.'

'What?' Like some sort of drop-in centre?' Said Margo, eyebrows raised her pregnancy bump preventing her from leaning fully towards me.

'Yes, I suppose, something like that.'

'Have you anywhere in mind?' I don't think around here would be suitable. There seems to be a coffee shop on every corner.'

'No, I did not mean here, as in the UK.'

'Oh, where else would it be?'

'Italy.'

'Italy?'

'Yes, in Portovenere.'

Margo was taken aback at my idea and I was unsure about it as well but when I was lying awake thinking about all the money I would have, why not but relocate to Italy? It was where I had felt a connection, where I seemed to have more friends than I had here. Margo was the only friend with whom I bothered to keep in touch and the weather was also a clincher. Although in Italy the winter would be cold especially near the sea, the summers were hot and glorious. I would have to brush up on my Italian and also import books in the language as not all people over there spoke English.

'Well, that is something to mull over,' said Margo.

'Of course, I would have to check everything out regarding development applications and zoning etc.'

'Of course,' Margo replied.

'But where would it be in Portovenere?'

'In the cottage, hopefully,' I replied surprised that I had actually verbalised it.

'The cottage?'

I detected a trace of doubt in her reply. It made me question if this plan of mine was a pie in the sky or would it come to fruition. What did I have to lose anyway? If I was unable to purchase the cottage and the development plan was rejected by the council, then that would be it and I would be no worse off than now. I would look into purchasing another property if not in Portovenere, then maybe one of the other villages in Cinque Terre. At least there was someone I knew on the council who might be helpful to my cause and I determined to contact him when I returned. We finished our drinks and made our way to a table where over racks of lamb, continued our conversation about the pros and cons of my endeavour, and the impending birth of Margo's second child.

Mr Cowdrey had suggested I should not rush into anything, just take my time as it was a lot to think about. It certainly was a lot to think about I mused, as I set about clearing out her apartment, placing her clothes, shoes and hats into plastic bags ready for the charity shop. Good old aunt, she had not been a bad old stick, although I had railed about her during her illness and now felt guilty about it. As I pulled another jacket from the hanger, I thought this was the second time I had been called upon to do this task. I was waiting for that ephemeral smell of old age which I had detected when clearing out mother's house but there was none. Perhaps it had been because aunt was not my mother that I could not detect anything, I was not so attuned or as sensitive towards aunt as I had been with mother. I thought of her now as I picked up a silver backed brush off the dressing table. Mother had possessed one and I had taken it home. As I had brushed my hair with our strands melded together I had an uncanny feeling of closeness to her reuniting us even though she was dead. I had been unable to discover anything more about her as the box of photos had not unearthed anything of significance. I was disappointed and felt rather let down but at least I had disposed of her ashes and stayed in the cottage which had been what she had wanted. I had resigned myself to her remaining a mystery.

I contacted the agent in Riomaggiore, advising him that I was waiting for my aunt's probate to go through. I told him of my intention to return to the cottage and I would cover whatever rent was due and owing. It took two months before I was able to cash in the blue stock shares and put the residence on the market. During that time, I had tendered my resignation from the library. They had been rather surprised at this surmising that I would be sorting and filing books until I was in my dotage. However, they understood about my need to move on and explore other opportunities, and I was sent off with a huge bunch of flowers and a bottle of shiraz. I signed with a Kensington agent who drove a Ferrari and advised I should expect a good price as the house was in an area which appealed to professional couples. I left the house as it was. Apart from a general clean, there was no need to change anything as the plush furnishings and decor attested to aunt's excellent taste. Then I contacted Maria and told her I was returning and booked a flight to Pisa from whence I would take the train to Cinque Terre.

It was a few days before I was due to depart that I received something in the mail. It was in an envelope on the front of which was the name of a legal firm, Crawley & Rowbottom which was unfamiliar as I had only had dealings with aunt's solicitor, Mr Cowdrey. I assumed it might be something to do with aunt's affairs, something about the shares or the sale of the house. I opened the envelope and the letter inside and read:

Dear Miss Banks,

Enclosed herewith please find correspondence from our client, the late Mrs Edwina Banks who wished us to forward to you after her death.

Please accept our sincere condolences and if you require any further assistance, please do not hesitate to contact the undersigned.

Yours faithfully,
Martin Crawley
Crawley & Rowbottom
Solicitors at Law

Why did mother engage these solicitors and instruct them to deliver this to me after her death? I could not fathom it and it was with a sense of foreboding I opened the envelope and read the enclosure.

My dearest pet,

I am doing what seems the best thing to do in the circumstances. You see I know I have a genetic cancer and I do not wish to undergo the suffering which awaits me.

I have given myself to the sea in which our favourite poet swam. You have given me much happiness in our time together my pet but now you are free to go to Tom and have his child.

Treasure our final days and the memories we shared and remember me if you ever return to the cottage.

PS. If my body is found it is my wish that my ashes be scattered near the grotto of Byron.

For the sword outwears its sheath,
And the soul wears out the breast,
And the hearth must pause to breathe,
And love itself have rest.

Harry

Shocked, I sat there for what seemed like an age with the letters in my lap. Mother had wanted me to know that she had a lover named Harry. He had committed suicide at Portovenere. He was the one with whom she had stayed at the cottage. She had been pregnant with me and Harry had wished her to return to Tom, my father, who had taken her back and tried to make the marriage succeed. Poor dad, he had been more or less cuckolded and had put up with mother's moods, staying with us and trying to do his best. It was so much to take in. I wondered if this Harry's body was ever recovered or had it disappeared into the depths of the inky sea, or been taken by sharks. To dilute the shock, I poured myself a double whisky then rang Margo who had been as astounded as I had when she heard the news.

'Oh Georgia,' she said. 'I'm so glad you now finally have closure. The mystery is solved. Now you can get on with your life in Italy and put all this behind you.'

I was grateful for her advice and would do as she suggested. The mystery had been solved and it was time to move on.

She came with Peter and Hamish to farewell me at Heathrow and amidst the laughter and a few tears I told them to come and visit if they had an opportunity. They could stay with me in the cottage if I was fortunate enough to purchase it, this cottage which now meant more to me than before. My flight was announced. With final hugs I navigated customs then boarded Air Italia to take me back to Italy and to the cottage on the cliff.

The flight time was two and a half hours and I settled back in my first-class seat being plied with Moet champagne and canapés of smoked salmon as we winged our way through fluffy clouds up and over the English Channel. I had always travelled economy class but now, thanks to aunt's legacy, there was more than enough money in the bank to treat myself to a bit of luxury. I could get used to this way of life I thought as the steward poured me another glass of Moet which I took with alacrity. I took a few sips then reached under the seat for my handbag. Prior to leaving for the airport the postman had delivered another envelope which was again from Crawley & Rowbottom. As I had not had time to read it, I had stuffed it into my bag intending to peruse it during the flight. I wondered what else they were sending me. After the last missive, surely there could not be any more momentous news for me to digest. I tore open the envelope. It was a letter with another enclosure.

Dear Miss Banks,

Enclosed herewith please find a letter from our client, the late Mrs Edwina Banks. Due to an administrative error, it was omitted from our previous correspondence.

Please accept our sincere apologies for this omission and if you require any further assistance, please do not hesitate to contact the undersigned.

Yours faithfully,
Martin Crawley
Crawley & Rowbottom
Solicitors at Law

Feeling rather miffed that the solicitors had omitted to forward this missive with the previous correspondence, I swallowed another good mouthful of champagne, opened the envelope addressed to me and commenced reading the enclosure.

Dearest Georgia,

By the time you read this letter I will be dead.

Now you are no longer a child, you will be perhaps able to understand life a little better, about relationships, affairs of the heart and all that entails.

I am sorry I was not a good mother or a good wife to your father who stood by me in my darkest hours and made sure you were cared for when I was incapable. You see, I had a lover named Harriette or Harry as I called her and she called me Ed. Harry and Ed. I met her at a grand country house in Scotland while staying there with your father. She was one of the louche London crowd, those people whom I told you about in the final years of my life. She seemed to cast a spell over me luring me in with her charm and slowly I fell in love with her. We seemed to share the same interests, mini breaks in the country, visiting historical sites and a love of poetry especially Byron's. I must have always had a predeliction for the opposite sex and did not know it until I met Harry. However, the relationship was complicated as I was still with your father and I spent many hours agonising over whom I should be with.

I was pregnant with you when Harry and I travelled to Italy and I am sure you were conceived on the same night when I met her. She must have known she was ill when she invited me to go with her and had planned to end her life in Portovenere where we stayed in a cottage over Byron's grotto. She threw herself off the cliff when I was dining with your father who had come to stay with us for a few days. I have enclosed the suicide note which she left for me and nobody but you has ever witnessed. She was my one true love and I never got over her death. My grief had been deep and I had periods of depression because I missed her so much. The grief was exacerbated when her body had been found washed up three weeks later at Palmaria, an island off Portovenere. An autopsy had been conducted and it was found that although her death had been deemed accidental a quantity of cocaine had been detected in her blood and a benign cyst located in her left breast. So, you see, she did not have cancer as she had thought and had killed herself for nothing. I used to imagine that my grief and sobs would affect you when you were forming in my womb. My disappointment would twist your features or your limbs into something resembling hate so you would be born strange. However, you were quite the opposite and I had been relieved when you were presented to me perfect in every way. In all the time we were married your father did not question me about my relationship with Harry but I am sure he must have known. He was a good man and did not deserve the angst through which I put him.

He and I were interviewed by the Italian police and cleared of any involvement. There was a notice inserted in the Daily Mail regarding her death and there was a bit of publicity to follow as Harriette was the daughter of the Labour Minister, Anthony Cavendish. Her wish for her ashes to be scattered in the sea could not be granted as her father had her remains flown back to the UK. She is buried in the cemetery at Highgate but I could never bring myself to visit her there. I preferred to remember her as she was when she was alive.

I do not expect you to forgive me for the way I treated you and your father but I wanted you to know the circumstances which led to my behaviour.

Your mother
Edwina

I sat in my seat absolutely stunned while tears poured down my cheeks. Just as I had been informed that mother had a lover, I now find out the lover was not a man but a woman! I thought of the photos I had discovered, the ones in the box. That woman who was at the picnic and sunbathing on the rocks had been mother's lover!

The woman next to me looked across clearly disturbed by my show of distress.

'Bad news?' She queried, removing her glasses and putting down her book.

'Oh, yes, sorry, you could say that.' I replied grabbing some tissues from my pocket and swiping at my face not caring if my mascara was running as that was the least of my concerns.

'Do you want to share?'

She was a woman of middle years with a kindly face, a stranger and I would not see her again. I needed to tell someone what I had just read to relieve me of this burden, this second shock, this bolt from the blue which had hit me like a hammer.

With trembling voice, thirty thousand feet in the air I told this woman in the first-class compartment of Air Italia about my quest to unearth my mother's history, the scattering of her ashes in the Ligurian sea at Portovenere, staying in the cottage on the cliff. I told her about the suicide note and read to her mother's letter to me from the grave. When I had completed my monologue, she had summoned the steward and ordered us glasses of brandy.

'Well, I must say,' she said after we had introduced each other. 'That is certainly a story. As a matter of fact, I think it should be in print.'

She informed me she was a literary agent and knew of a few authors who would be able to ghost write such a story if I was agreeable to pay whatever charges would be applicable. She even had a title, Return to Portovenere. That was the third shock, mother's story in print! She gave me her business card and told me to contact her if I decided to pursue her proposal.

Fortified by champagne and brandy, it was however with a mixture of emotions that I stepped from the plane in Pisa and made my way to the station where a train awaited to transport me back to Cinque Terre. Settled in my first-class seat, my mind was laden as the train rushed through the tunnels and the tiny villages clinging to the cliffs. I was trying to process everything, trying to have empathy with my mother, putting myself in her position, trying to find forgiveness for the way she had treated my father. I thought of the agent's suggestion. It would make a decent story, perhaps be cathartic, and expunge the thoughts which jostled in my head. How ironic was it that I happened to be seated next to such an amiable person who was a literary agent and I had the confidence to recount everything to her?

We arrived at Riomaggiore. I boarded the ferry, the same one I had taken all those months ago. It seemed much longer, so much had happened in the interim, especially in the last few days. The ancient steeple of San Pietro loomed in the distance. It seemed to beckon me, to give me succour. I would again pray in that church as I had the day when mother's ashes were scattered. I would pray for compassion towards mother and her lover, Harry and mostly I would pray for my father who had stepped into the breach and through adversity, had kept us all together.

The ferry hove into the wharf and I was here, I had returned to Portovenere. I could see my friends, Maria and Piero frantically waving to me. Their loud exclamations of 'Buongiorno, benvenuto' echoing across the sea and over the gulf of poets.

Epilogue

After a whirlwind romance Ernest married his Italian sweetheart, Giovanna in Pisa where in their wedding finery with much hilarity they were photographed trying to hold up the ancient tower. After many negotiations, she had finally obtained a settlement with her ex-husband who agreed to give her the apartment in Sienna. Ernest resigned from his job in Fleet Street and studied Italian. As he and Giovanna both hankered for the countryside, they decided to sell the apartment and relocated to Monte Amiata. Giovanna swapped her high heels and couture dresses for wellington boots as they had bought a farm which bred Cinta Senese pigs. They learnt about the husbandry of them, the production of the pork sausages and parma ham which they sold to the local community and to the travellers who passed through as Ernest regaled the customers with the stories he had covered, especially the one in Portovenere.

After some persuasion, Ernest's mother moved with Bernie into one of the new council houses which Ernest had purchased for them. It was just down the street from their old miner's cottage and his mother enjoyed showing off her new abode to the neighbours who popped in for cups of tea and scones. There was a garden where Bernie could sit in his wheelchair especially when the sun was out. He could watch the village activity, the birds flying about and the bees pollinating the flowers.

Giovanna had given birth to six children, four boys and two girls and Ernest's suspicions about her ex-husband had been correct as he was found to have mafia associations. He was fatally stabbed during a brawl amongst the grapes of a Tuscan vineyard. Giovanna had not held back with her condemnation of him and the pigs' ears burned with the many 'testa di cazzo' expletives which flew around the farm.

Georgia's suspicions about the Filipino nurse had also proved correct, as she had been found guilty of administering a fatal overdose of insulin to two patients in a nursing home in Hammersmith and now was incarcerated in Wormwood Scrubs prison.

Applications to the Cinque Terre Council had been successful although there was an interminable amount of waiting as the Italian bureaucracy was not known for its expediency. However, now the cottage on the cliff is a community centre. There are new and used books for sale, coffee, tea and light snacks are served and two days a week a psychologist/counsellor from Sienna attends to assist with relationship problems or other concerns. The delay had been worthwhile in the end, as Georgia was able to extend and reconfigure the cottage to accommodate the centre, herself and her loving partner, Judy, the author of Return to Portovenere. It was published to high acclaim and negotiations are under way for the production of a screenplay to be filmed on site.

THE END

MORE BOOKS PUBLISHED BY PHAROS BOOKS

DARK PSYCHOLOGY Secrets & MANIPULATION
AMY BROWN

NLP Secrets
AMY BROWN

eBook available

AVAILABLE ON
amazon.in
Flipkart

✉ sales@pharosbooks.in 📞 011 40395855 🌐 www.pharosbooks.in

Plot No..-55, Main Mother Dairy Road, Pandav Nagar, East Delhi-110092

BOOKS PUBLISHED BY PHAROS BOOKS

JANE EYRE — Charlotte Bronte	**HOW TO STOP WORRYING & START LIVING** — Dale Carnegie	**HINDU DHARMA** — M. K. Gandhi	**GULLIVER'S TRAVELS** — Jonathan Swift
Grimm's Fairy Tales — The Brothers Grimm	**GREAT EXPECTATIONS** — Charles Dickens	**FOR THE TERM OF HIS NATURAL LIFE** — Marcus Clarke	**EMMA** — Jane Austen
DUBLINERS — James Joyce	**DRACULA** — Bram Stoker	**Down and Out in Paris and London**	**Bleak House** — Charles Dickens
The Autobiography of BENJAMIN FRANKLIN	**AROUND THE WORLD IN 80 DAYS** — Jules Verne	**Anne of Green Gables**	**Alice's Adventures in Wonderland** — Lewis Carroll

sales@pharosbooks.in 011-40395855 www.pharosbooks.in

A-55, Main Mother Dairy Road, Pandav Nagar, East Delhi-110092

Printed in the USA
CPSIA information can be obtained
at www.ICGtesting.com
LVHW081204130224
771720LV00007B/748

9 789395 862370